ENCORES

A Novel by
Russell Róbe

ALMUS
PUBLICATIONS

Almus Publications, LLC
Medford, Oregon

(almuspublications.com)

Table of Contents

What If?

Except for a few historical details, *Encores* depicts characters who have never lived, places that have never existed, events that never occurred, and conversations that were never uttered. All of these, as they appear in this volume of interconnected short stories, are solely products of the author's imagination.

Encores is an exercise in wildly creative fiction. It's a quirky, whimsical mixture of speculative history, futuristic fantasy, and curious scenarios in an eternity where musicians and listeners alike are gifted with true immortality. It's a setting that compels us to ask: What if there were an afterlife? What if our physical bodies were permanently restored to their youthful prime? What if there were chances to move beyond all the regretful errors we've ever made? What if eternity and resurrection could breathe life into musical might-have-beens and should-have-beens? What if music's lost potential and the fullness of its destiny could be realized in endless encores that are majestically yet to be?

Chapter 1: Greg and Sue

Music is, to me, proof of the existence of God.
It is so extraordinarily full of magic.
Kurt Vonnegut Jr.

Hamburg, Germany – March 1978

"Just follow the goat turds."

Sure enough, there was a sporadic trail of unmistakable black goat droppings leading down a dark, narrow corridor, around a left turn, up two steps, down a shorter stretch of hallway, then up five more steps to a small landing where Greg and his bandmates were to await their turn. On stage at the small club was a slender young blonde woman with a dark wool cap reading her poetry into a microphone. Tethered to one of her denim belt loops was a wide-bellied goat patiently facing the audience while a pile of droppings steadily accumulated behind.

When Greg's band took the stage a short time later, the spit began to fly through the air like a howling blizzard. There didn't seem to be any anger or displeasure behind this display, but the tens of punk rockers pressing up against the stage had begun to spit back and forth in every direction. By the end of the band's first tune, Greg had to wipe his face and guitar with a towel.

"Let's kick it up a notch," he turned and said to the band. "Skip *Remember* and take it from *Cold Hard Cash*." The other three musicians quickly glanced down at their set lists taped to the stage floor.

Moments later, the audience was riveted. Then dancing. Then cheering. Time evaporated in an instant, and the set seemed to end way too quickly. The applause, yelling, and whistling started out remarkably loud, and yet its intensity only grew between the first, second, and third encore numbers. The crowd begged for more, but The Greg Kihn Band soon slipped out the backstage door having conquered another European audience.

******

San Francisco Bay Area – April 1979

"Yeah, the top three show bands you'll ever see are The Rolling Stones, Bruce Springsteen, and Greg Kihn," said Tom. His buddy Ed nodded in agreement. Both of them were sound and stage technicians who worked with a wide assortment of venues and bands throughout the Bay Area. And when they weren't working, they were concertgoers who had seen every big-name gig that ever played in California, some of them multiple times.

I had just met Tom and Ed through a mutual friend and was intrigued by their confident assessment. By that time, the end of the 1970s, most everyone from great-grandparents to preschoolers had heard of The Stones. And the impressive growth of Springsteen's fanbase was showing no signs of winding down. But, The Greg Kihn Band? Who had ever heard of them?

"They're big here in the Bay Area," answered Tom.

"And in Europe," added Ed.

"But they haven't really taken off anywhere else yet for some reason," Tom went on.

"Why is that?" I asked.

"I don't know," said Tom, "but they're rockers. They'll get a crowd going like no one else."

I liked the sound of that. Good music gave me life and fed my soul, and when combined with the ability to entertain, well, this world didn't have too much better to offer.

"They're playing up at Chico State in a few weeks – at the Pioneer Days show," said Ed. "Tom's doing sound for them."

"I can't get you in backstage," Tom quickly interjected, "but it'll be worth the drive up there."

2

In those days, long before the Internet and social media, a tip like that was highly valued and appreciated. And going to see a show in Chico was also an opportunity to make amends with my dear friend Sue.

All I can say is that I blew it. I mean, I had a new girlfriend for a few weeks there, so what could I do? But, looking back on my close, family-like relationship with Sue and her mom, I maybe should have picked up on their down-to-the-wire hints and invited Sue to her senior prom. Instead, I went to a movie with my girlfriend, and Sue stayed home that night. She was class president, and she stayed home that night – because all the other guys assumed she had already been asked to the prom. And they probably all thought I was the one who had asked her. Sue and her mom never said anything about their disappointment with my blindness and insensitivity, but I could tell our since-childhood friendship had taken a big, sad hit.

"So, I'm going to Chico this weekend. Do you want to come along?" I eventually asked Sue over the phone.

"Are you going to Pioneer Days?" she asked, referring to the town's annual history celebration that included an all-day music fest.

"Yeah, I want to see the show on Saturday. There's supposed to be some good bands there this year." Sue didn't bother asking me about the lineup. She was mostly just interested in a fun day together, especially if it involved music.

It was good to have the windows down, driving north through the backroads, passing all the orchards and fruit stands on the way up to Chico. The wind whipped through our hair while my car's eight-track tape player cranked Boston, Little River Band, Electric Light Orchestra, and Queen. It was inevitable that *Bohemian Rhapsody* should start sounding through my custom homemade speakers.

"Mama. Just killed a man–" sang Freddie Mercury mournfully.

"Do you think he really did it?" Sue asked me loudly, through the music and the air rushing past the windows.

"Did what?" I asked, just as loudly.

"You know – killed some guy," she responded.

"Freddie Mercury?? I don't think so! Even the police officers in England aren't allowed to carry handguns," I stated with confidence.

"Makes you wonder though," she went on. "What was he singing about then? I mean, why else did he write those words, you think? What else could they mean?"

"I don't know. Maybe it's like one of those things … What are they called? … Parables, I think. Anyway, it's like when you're telling a story about one thing, but really, it's about something else. Supposed to be kind of poetic, I guess."

"Whenever I hear this song," replied Sue, "I start thinking about this life and then how it eventually ends and stuff. Like, what happens after? I'm thinking we don't just completely disappear, right?"

"What do you mean?" I asked.

"It's true that we're sitting here talking, right? We both know that we exist right now. How does that knowledge or existence ever come to an end? It just seems like it has to keep going forever somehow."

"You mean like we keep on living after we're dead?" I asked. I hadn't given any serious thought about the afterlife since I quit going to church a couple years earlier.

"Well, we all have memories," said Sue. "I mean, I have vivid memories from when we were little kids, and those memories are alive still, even though I'm not a little kid anymore. Maybe there's like this big memory bank out there that you can just tap into forever and that's how you keep going."

Sue started to giggle as these ideas tumbled out of her mouth. She was always having funny thoughts about the mysteries of life and beyond. As for me at that age, I was just looking for good times with some good tunes and my good

4

friend Sue. And I knew it was going to be a good time at the Pioneer Days show that afternoon.

Sammy Hagar was the headliner that day and so, understandably, when an unknown long-hair band from L.A. opened the show, they were politely received by the mostly metalhead crowd. But when The Greg Kihn Band took the stage next, the scene changed dramatically. With a notably modern/retro look and shorter hairstyles that reflected recent touring in Europe, they did not receive such a warm welcome. The first notes weren't even struck before the booing began and garbage started to fly.

"Oh, no! Did you see that?" asked Sue, with a peculiar mix of concern and anxiety.

Cups and wadded up paper bags littered the air, and a Coke bottle had just missed Dave, the guitarist.

"Man!" I replied. "This could get ugly!"

The band stood firm though, smiling even, working their way through the steady drive of their music. By the end of the second tune, the garbage had stopped flying, and the audience's attention was fixed on the fresh new faces. It wasn't metal, but the music was good – really good.

By the fourth tune, that same garbage-throwing audience was up on their feet, dancing and jumping to the music of those shorter-haired guys from Berkeley. And, once again, the set came to an all-too-sudden end. The crowd wouldn't let Greg and the boys leave the stage. There were one, two, then three encore numbers to answer the ongoing applause. The miraculous transformation gave me and Sue goosebumps, and we would talk about that powerful show long afterward.

That trip to Chico marked a new beginning of many good times for Sue and me. We were still just friends, nothing romantic at all, but we got the most out of our new appreciation of Greg Kihn and his band. They had regular gigs at both of the Bay Area's Keystone clubs, and places like The Old Waldorf, plus there were a few free, weekday summer shows in San Francisco. Sue and I would both call in

sick on those days. And there was Greg up on that stage –
always working the crowd, building up tension, letting it go,
building it up again into a great rocking crescendo. All the
while he'd be singing and strumming and rhythmically
nodding his head in positive affirmation of his music's
power. Along with the rest of the fans, we were hooked.

******

San Francisco Bay Area – August 2012

More than thirty years later and many hundreds of miles
away from that time and place found me on the phone with
another old friend named Ellen, whose number I managed to
locate.

"Well, one reason I called," I said, "is that I'm going to
be in town this weekend. I know it's kind of last-minute, but
I thought maybe we could get the old gang together for
dinner at Skipolini's or something."

"Oh, that would be wonderful," said Ellen. "It has been
such a long time!"

It *had* been such a long time. I'm sad to say that the
previous decades, with their college, marriage, kids, jobs, and
travels distracted me from keeping in touch with my old
friends. I hadn't seen or talked to them since the old days –
not even Sue. It was time for me to try mending that
relationship once again. But the upcoming opportunity
suddenly looked like it might slip away altogether.

"Uh, I should probably tell you that Sue might not be
able to join us," said Ellen.

"Why's that?" I asked vaguely, thinking some other
appointment or travels might already have claimed Sue's
time.

"Oh, … that's right. Maybe you haven't heard."

"About what? What's going on?" I asked.

"Well, Sue's been dealing with leukemia the last little
while and–"

"Oh, no … I had no idea!"

"Yeah, yeah. It's been pretty rough. She's doing chemo right now and all that. She has some up days, but a lot more down days."

"Man, I can't believe this ... Well, uh, tell her I'll be in town. I'd love to see her."

"I know she'd love to see you too," said Ellen. "You remember her brother Rob, right? She's staying at his place in Berkeley. He's out of town for a few days, and I'm staying there with Sue this weekend. How about if you meet us there and we can get together with the others the next time you're in town?"

"Do you think it would be okay for me to see her now?" I asked. "I mean, would Sue mind me seeing her when she's ill like this?"

"Are you kidding? Sue? You know she doesn't care about stuff like that. Of course, she'd love to see you again. But, I should let you know, she doesn't look well. So just act like she does, and she'll be thrilled.

"Got it. How does Saturday afternoon sound?"

"That would be great!" said Ellen.

The call came to an end, and I sat there for a long silent time in a mild state of shock, occasionally shaking my head and whispering to myself. Sue was seriously ill. Unbelievable! I thought about giving her a call but figured it would be best to meet with Sue in person first after all these years.

Driving through Berkeley that Saturday afternoon got me reliving all the good times and shows Sue and I had experienced together. I arrived at the place and knocked lightly on the apartment door. I felt little chills going through me as I anticipated a happy reunion, but some of them came from my uncertainty about Sue's health and appearance.

Ellen answered the door delighted to see me but quickly stepped outside and closed the door behind her for a private word.

"So good to see you, Lawrence!" she said through a big, long hug.

"And you too, Ellen!" I responded in kind.

"Before we go in," said Ellen, pulling back from the embrace, "I need to tell you, it's not looking good. The leukemia and the treatments have really taken a toll on Sue. She's going in for more tests on Monday, but there's only so much more medication she can take. They're worried about possible kidney failure. I just wanted to warn you."

Ellen started to push the door back open, and I could see a frail figure sitting in a recliner chair. She was wearing a pastel yellow robe and was crowned with a creamy white headcover. Of course, it was Sue. As I moved closer, her eyes widened, and a genuine smile spread across her face, but I could tell that her greeting took some exertion through weakness and pain.

"Oh, Lawrence!" she said softly as I put my arms around her shoulders. She could barely return the gesture, lightly touching my elbows with her fingertips while she shook slightly with small sobs. I eventually drew back to look into her wet eyes. Ellen thoughtfully handed her a tissue.

"I'm a mess," said Sue in a tiny, scratchy voice, as she gently dabbed her eyes. There was something in her tone that suggested a laughing, humorous apology.

"Oh, you look wonderful," I responded, shrugging off her comment. Her skin had a greenish, translucent tone, almost as if she had been embalmed. "I'm just so happy to see you again."

"I can't believe you're here, Lawrence. It's been so long."

"Way too long," I replied. "I'm sorry about all that."

"It's alright," she said in a near whisper, "I'm just glad you're here, back in the Bay Area. Remember that laser show in San Francisco?"

"Oh yeah," I said, recalling the distant memory. "Some new FM station had their music synched up to different colored laser beams shining patterns on the clouds one summer night."

"We sat on a big blanket on the hillside," added Sue, "not far from Coit Tower."

"Yeah, I remember that," I said.

"And you always will. It's part of your memory bank," said Sue with a smile. "You'll be able to keep that memory forever. I know I will."

For a moment, I was tempted to ask Sue if she still believed in some sort of afterlife but thought better of it. It seemed as if that threshold might not be too far away for her.

"You know," she went on, "there were times when the music at some concerts was so good I wondered if God was there too."

"What do you mean? Sitting right there next to us, enjoying the show?"

"Yeah, why not?" Sue replied softly. "I mean, he makes this world, and makes all these people, and the people make all this good music. You don't think he's there sometimes? Just listening, like a parent enjoying their kid's piano recital?"

"He would sort of stand out in the crowd, don'tcha think?" I asked humorously.

"No, he'd be there incognito, hiding in plain sight. And he'd always get the best seats – for free," Sue laughed. "I know that's what *I* would be doing all the time if I were a god."

Ellen brought me a chair so I could sit closer to Sue. For an hour or so, we sat there, a lot of it in silence while I held her cold hand on the armrest, and her eyes periodically closed at length. When there was talking to be done, I did most of it – not asking Sue too many questions so as not to drain her limited energies. When I did ask her questions, most of them began with, "Remember that time...?" and mostly she would just nod her head and smile in response.

"Remember that time we went to the Pioneer Days show in Chico?"

"Greg Kihn," she replied with a smile.

"We saw that band quite a few times, didn't we?"

9

"I loved those free lunchtime concerts in the summer," she said, "right in front of the Ferry Building in San Francisco. It's like I can still smell the waterfront when I think about it. I'll never forget those days."

Sue and I went on talking about Greg Kihn shows and other concerts a while longer before Ellen wisely determined, for Sue's sake, that a break was needed. She dropped the hint with a question of her own for Sue. "Do you need to lie down for a little bit?"

"Soon," said Sue.

"Lawrence," said Ellen, "there's a deli just down the block. Do you think you could go pick up some crunchy chicken salad?"

"Of course," I replied, taking both the hint and the suggestion that I was welcome back at the apartment for a short time following my errand. "Sue, can I get you anything?"

"A little 7-Up, please," she said softly, barely raising her hand from the armrest and holding her thumb and index finger slightly apart.

Ellen followed me out the door, and I was glad she did so I could express some concerns about Sue.

"Why didn't you tell me she was in such bad shape?" I asked.

"Well, I told you she has ups and downs that come and go, and this is a bad day, I guess. But she has just lit up since you arrived. She's so happy to see you."

"Lit up? Man, how did she look before I arrived? I mean, shouldn't she be in the hospital or something?"

"I told you, there's not much that can be done at this point."

"But, can't we–"

"Listen," Ellen interrupted, "right now Sue's comfortable, she's happy, and this afternoon she's got the company of two dear friends. Anyway, a home health provider will be here later this evening to check on her. Now, why don't you go and get that crunchy chicken salad? Then you can visit with Sue a little while longer."

The bells on the door gave a jingle when I walked into the deli. The only other customer, a man with his back to me, had just placed his order.

"To go, please," I heard him say to the lady behind the counter.

"Be right with you," she announced to me without looking up. While she was putting the man's order together, I glanced around the room and took in all the nostalgia. There were framed concert posters and notices from the 1960s, 70s, and 80s all over the walls. I smiled as I reflected on a few of those shows I had been to myself, some of them with Sue.

My eyes paused at a club flier featuring Greg Kihn. I couldn't remember if Sue and I had gone to that particular show, but I debated whether to ask the deli's manager if I could buy the framed flier. It would be such a nice present to bring back to the apartment for Sue.

As I stood there with my head aimed upward at the poster, a gravelly voice behind me said, "Those were the days, huh?"

I turned around to face the other customer, an older gentleman, shorter than me, with a dignified appearance.

"Yes, those were some days," I said, adding, "I met him once."

"Who?" asked the gentleman.

"Greg Kihn … uh … of The Greg Kihn Band." I added that last detail, pointing up at the poster, thinking the man seemed too old to know of such things. 'After his time' were the words that passed through my mind. "Yeah, I even stole a towel from him once," I said, laughing over the sudden memory and over how ridiculous my blurted confession must have sounded.

"What?" asked the man, offering a rough chuckle of his own. "Now that's a story I'd like to hear!"

"Here you go, sir," said the lady behind the counter, handing a full paper sack to the gentleman. "And what can I get for you?" she asked, now looking directly at me.

"How about a pound and a half of your crunchy chicken salad?"

"We're making some fresh in the back right now if you can wait a few minutes."

"Sure. That's fine," I said.

"So, now, what was the deal? You say you stole a towel from that guy?" asked the older man, still standing near me with his paper sack in hand. He seemed genuinely interested in continuing our conversation, and having gotten my attention back, nodded toward a nearby table and began moving that direction. I instinctively felt comfortable sharing an old memory or two with this amused stranger, so I joined him at the table.

As we both sat down, I continued, "Yeah, I got this chance one night to be backstage for one of his shows at the Keystone club, the one down in Palo Alto. So, I'm just hanging out there, mostly watching the band from the side of the stage, and I just can't believe I made it back there, you know?"

"You had never been backstage at a show before?" asked the man.

"No, and I never have since. And I never felt so cool in my whole life. Like I was somebody!"

The man gave an appreciative, gravelly chuckle.

"And so, when the band finishes their set, I kind of follow them backstage again – but, keeping my distance a bit, trying not to act like a groupie, right? But I'm just thrilled to be there, and I can see the band sitting in this little dressing room lounge with the door open. The crowd is still clapping and yelling and stuff, and the band's just sitting there, taking a little break before they head back out for an encore. They weren't in there more than a minute or so, but I remember Steve the bass player saying something like, 'Make 'em work for it!' Anyway, just then, I see Greg Kihn pick up this little white towel and wipe his forehead, and then he sets it down on a table as they all got up and headed back to the stage."

"So, let me guess ... They left that dressing room door open, right?" asked the man with a big grin.

"Yeah, and I was reminded of some Beatlemania craze years earlier where bits of hotel towel supposedly used by John Lennon or Paul McCartney were auctioned off for lots of money."

"You were going to sell that towel?!" asked the man in disbelief.

"No, no!" I said, laughing. "My friend Sue was a big Greg Kihn fan, and I thought I would bring her that sweaty towel back from the show as sort of a Beatles-like joke. So, I just walked straight into that dressing room, grabbed that little towel, and stuck it in my pocket."

"And what did Sue think about that?"

"She thought it was hilarious! Promised never to wash it and all that. Unfortunately, her mom tossed the towel in the laundry a couple weeks later – she didn't know what it was. Sue and I joked about that for a long time. In fact, we were just laughing about that story a few minutes ago."

The older man's shoulders shook a little with an inner laugh, and then he sat there for a while, looking down, as if not knowing what to make of my strange story. Finally, he looked up again, straight into my eyes and asked, "You said this was at the Keystone?"

"Yes," I responded, "the one down in Palo Alto."

"Hmmm," he said after another pause, "I always wondered what happened to that towel."

My eyes locked into his as I tried to comprehend his words. Did I know him from someplace? The aged man before me bore no resemblance to anyone I had ever seen before. Not a trace. Except maybe something about those eyes, a look enhanced by a widening grin on his face.

"What do you mean?" I finally asked, utterly perplexed.

He didn't respond right away, but the grin kept getting bigger. It couldn't be. There's no way!

"I said, I always wondered what happened to my towel."

"You're not–?"

"Oh, come on, man! Do I really look that old?"

"Are you–"

"Roadrunner, Roadrunner, going faster miles an hour," he started to sing in a similarly unrecognizable voice. "Yeah, I'm Greg Kihn! And I want my towel back!" he blurted, interrupting his raspy singing with a loud, raspy laugh.

I was still having trouble putting the whole picture together in my mind. Some people just look like an older version of themselves as they age, but I would never have guessed this man to be the youthful Greg Kihn I had seen perform so many years before. But as his head began to nod in affirmation of his words, I caught a glimpse of the old days. And I believed him. I believed the unthinkable because it was true. I was sitting in a Berkeley deli talking to Greg Kihn!

As soon as I was able to gather my thoughts I said, "Well, I'm sure Sue still has your towel, and she's only a short walk from here."

"Aw, I'm just joking with you, buddy. I actually never missed that towel at all."

"Yeah, but … could you come with me for just a few minutes and say hi to her? Look, I normally wouldn't dare to even ask something like this, but it's just too much of a coincidence, that you're here … and … and … she doesn't have too much longer."

"What do you mean?"

"She doesn't have much time left. She's seriously ill. It would just mean so much if you could–"

"Oh, I don't know if–"

"Please, just for a couple minutes. She's just halfway down the block. If you could stop by with me and say hello, it would mean so much to her."

He looked down again but nodded his head in agreement. If Greg Kihn had enjoyed any entertainment success in his life, it had come from making his fans a top priority.

I paid for the salad and a bottle of 7-Up. The bells on the door rang again as Greg and I left the deli together.

Ellen answered the apartment door, and I quickly whispered, "I've brought someone to see Sue."

"What?? Who??!" Ellen asked with her eyebrows drawn together in concern. "Sue's in bed, already. Who is it?"

"You won't believe this, but I've got Greg Kihn with me. We'll just have him say hi to her for a minute, that's all."

"You've gotta be kidding! Greg Kihn??"

Greg was growing increasingly uncomfortable with the situation while standing there with me in the doorway, but Ellen relented, and soon Greg and I were standing at Sue's bedside. Her eyes were closed.

"Sue. Are you awake?" I asked quietly.

"Yes," she said softly without opening her eyes.

"I've brought someone to see you. He'd like to say hello."

Sue did not respond immediately. It was as if she were drifting in and out of deep sleep.

"It's Greg Kihn," I said. "I've brought Greg Kihn over to see you."

Sue's eyes remained closed, but she smiled, thinking I was joking with her.

"Hello Sue," said Greg. "I understand you've been to one or two of my shows."

At the sound of the unfamiliar voice, Sue opened her eyes to look at the visitor. She did not recognize the man standing next to me, nor his rough voice, but she also knew I would never extend a joke so far as to bring an imposter over for a visit.

"It's true," I said. "This is Greg Kihn. Can you believe it? We just met at the deli, and I brought him over to say hello."

"We went to your shows all the time," said Sue faintly, trying to sit up a bit.

"That's what I hear," said Greg. "I'm always happy to meet up with a fan." He noticed an acoustic guitar standing in a nearby corner. "Would you mind if I played you a song?"

Without waiting for an answer, Greg grabbed the guitar and pulled a nearby chair up to Sue's bedside. He gave the instrument a couple quick test strums and tightened a few of the strings. Then he gave it a couple more quick strums, seemed satisfied, and pulled the guitar's body in tight under his arm. He leaned closer to Sue, looking her in the eye as the rhythmic chords and lyrics started flowing.

"I came for you, for you. I came for you, but you did not heed my urgency," were the words Greg sang in a voice that suddenly sounded more youthful, and less ravaged by time. There was no doubt in Sue's mind that this was indeed Greg Kihn, and with that confirmation came acknowledgment of this magical, miraculous moment. The odds against it happening seemed astronomical.

Sue smiled, turned to look at me as I stood on the other side of the bed, and held out her hand. Kneeling, I took it in both of mine and was surprised at its temperature, even lower than before. As Greg continued to sing his tune from those bygone days, Sue closed her eyes again and saw swirling all around her, visions and memories of us together – when energy and health and confidence abounded, and when the cares of this world were practically unknown. And I knew this because, somehow, I could feel and see it all too as her hand slightly tightened its grip on mine. We were both caught in a hazy, slow-moving whirlpool where past and future seemed all mixed together, and where moments of light and darkness chased each other, and sensations of joy and rebirth softly came and went.

If Greg and Ellen were experiencing all of this too, I couldn't tell. I just know that Greg's tune smoothly transitioned into another old favorite as the music carried Sue through a transition of her own.

"Did you see that?" Sue whispered to me. I nodded. There was Dave the guitarist ducking a Coke bottle as garbage flew through the air. Steve was wiping the spit from his bass guitar. And drummer Larry was double-checking his set list taped to the floor. But then the crowd started cheering as the band worked their way through the set, and everyone was dancing. There were thousands of them. Thousands upon thousands of people – millions of them even – dancing and singing along with Greg, and yet awaiting his future arrival in their post-mortal realm.

"Remember, do you? Surrender, do you?" Greg sang there in the room, smiling and nodding along to his soft guitar rhythms. Sue nodded in reply and smiled to herself, with eyes still closed. And she did surrender, letting her existence in this life slip away into the next. Her hand loosened in mine as she left her pain and discomfort behind and joined the cheering, dancing crowd.

Chapter 2: No Escape from Reality

I think people should just listen to
[Bohemian Rhapsody], think about it, and then make
up their own minds as to what it says to them.
Freddie Mercury

Stone Town, Zanzibar – January 1964

Everything suddenly became much darker, and Aboud's ears were still ringing. Actually, it wasn't a ringing of the ears at all. It was more like an ongoing, residual memory of their ringing from a sharp blast just seconds before. Amazingly, he was still standing, or so it appeared, with bent knees lowered halfway into a squatting position. Incredulously, he raised his hand to the side of his head but felt nothing. Not just the absence of a wound, but nothing. Nothing at all. Fingertips seemingly met temple but neither surface acknowledged the presence of the other. The only thing Aboud could feel was a diminishing sense of self – slipping and floating and gently spinning, deep into a darker and darker state of near oblivion. Emptiness. Nothingness.

Inches away, and yet now worlds apart, Farookh stood there trembling, breathing rapidly, holding a tiny pistol in the palm of his hand. At his feet lay the wilting body of Aboud with a small but visible wound to the side of his head and his hand's tight grip on his sharp machete still loosening. A mixture of relief and shock rushed through Farookh's being. The immediate threat was now gone!

His eyes quickly shifted from Aboud's body to the pistol, and then upwards to a brightly lit, third-story window in the narrow Stone Town alleyway. In its frame was the silhouette of a man wearing glasses. The man stepped out of view. The room behind the window went completely dark.

Farookh continued to suck in short, shallow breaths one after the other. What had the man seen? Did he recognize Farookh? Did he witness the entire altercation? Or, had he only observed that final moment when Farookh fired his gun? Relief immediately gave way to fearing the potentially horrific consequences of killing one of the African revolutionaries. Farookh broke into a panicked sprint down the alleyway toward home.

How could life have turned upside down so rapidly? Just a few weeks before, in early December, there seemed to be only clear skies and sunshine as Zanzibar approached its hottest days of the year. Farookh and several newfound friends felt the warm midday air ripple through their hair and against their clothes as they gleefully bicycled over twenty miles to the island's eastern coastal village of Chwaka.

The plan for the bicycle ride had been hatched at Stone Town's Starehe Club, located between Zanzibar's British and American consulate buildings. The club had long been a coastal resort for pale, foreign visitors wanting to relax in warm, tropical breezes. From his earliest years, Farookh could recall groups of tipsy English tourists singing seaside vacation ditties there.

The back of the Starehe Club opened to a pristine, white sand beach with picturesque fishermen's canoes and dhows sailing just beyond. Farookh and his friends would often go swimming at the club, usually without showing much interest in its foreign patrons. That changed one afternoon with a question from a lanky, blond American boy sitting on the beach with a small group of compatriots.

"Hey! What do you do for fun on this island?" he asked as Farookh passed by. The other teens quietly laughed at the sassiness of the question posed so abruptly to a local stranger of ambiguous Asian descent. Farookh, swimming alone that day, had been intent on heading home just then but the spirited group caught his attention. He had never talked to Americans before and stopped to make their acquaintance.

"I'm Jim," said the blond boy, standing up and sticking out his hand in greeting, "but my friends call me Hoople." The others laughed again, this time over the funny sounding nickname.

"I'm Farookh," came the reply as the two shook hands, "but my friends sometimes call me Freddie." The teens chuckled once more, surprised to be having this fun exchange in English.

"So, you want to know what we do for fun here in Zanzibar?" Farookh continued. "Well, I'll tell you. Besides swimming in the sea, we go bicycle riding."

"To where?" asked Jim.

"To Chwaka, on the other side of the island," answered Farookh.

"And what do you do there in Chwaka?" asked Jim's sister, Patricia.

"We go swimming in the sea!" answered Farookh with a big smile, causing the group to laugh again.

Before long, plans and arrangements were made for the group of seven teens – four boys and three girls – to ride rented bicycles across Zanzibar's largest island. It was a sunny, breezy day filled with many stops along the surprisingly well-kept roads. Following behind the group with Jim, seventeen-year-old Farookh could not help but notice the size and shape of the American girls' posteriors centered upon their bicycles' seats. They seemed so much larger than those of all the young Persian, Indian, and Arab females he'd ever known. "Fat-bottomed girls," he laughed to himself and mentally gave Patricia the suitably round nickname, *Peaches*.

Workers in the countryside's spice farm fields would wave as they went by. Crows and pigeons occasionally flapped overhead. There was picnicking, volleyball, and tree climbing. Not surprisingly, the group also went swimming and wading in Chwaka's shallow coastal waters.

"Do you know the road to Tunguu village?" Jim asked Farookh later in the afternoon. "If we can stop by there on the way home, I'll show you where our father works."

More than halfway back to Stone Town, the group of young cyclists stopped near Tunguu, hoping to gain entrance to NASA's Mercury tracking station there. For security and reasons of politeness (accompanied as they were by one non-American), the teens were not allowed inside the facility's front gate that day. However, Jim and Patricia's father, Robert Morritsen, was delighted by his children's surprise visit and came out to greet the group. Mr. Morritsen, a NASA engineer, took the opportunity to point out some of the station's exterior features and recount its brief history.

"As some of you might know," he said, "this place was built a few years ago, in 1960. It's just one of several NASA stations located around the globe. It allows us to track orbits and communicate with the astronauts on our Mercury space flights." To Farookh there was an intriguing mystique to the word *Mercury* which fit perfectly with the modern, super-sonic marvel of people flying through space.

"Not everybody here is happy with the station though," Mr. Morritsen went on. "Why, just last July, during the local elections, the Afro-Shirazi Party claimed that this was really a U.S. military facility in disguise. They were saying it could be used to send missiles raining down onto Zanzibar. I'm not sure what we'd be interested in bombing here though. Coconut trees?"

Everyone but Farookh chuckled at the improbability. He was too enraptured by the sterile aluminum building behind the barbed-wire fence. It gleamed in the afternoon sunlight and its nearby radio tower was loaded with fantastic, complex gadgetry. Nothing about the place bore a resemblance to any structure Farookh had ever seen in his life. It was also the first time he had heard any hint of political tensions on what he had always thought to be a peaceful island. But in fact, Zanzibar's history had been anything but peaceful for many of its inhabitants. In the coming days, there would be an unexpected revolution, as its sudden, surprising rash of violence demanded repayment of history's debts.

On the largest of the Zanzibar's equatorial islands, just off Africa's eastern coastline, is a westward protrusion of land that juts out into the Indian Ocean. Upon that headland sits Zanzibar City, and at its pointy tip is the city's old historic sector known as Stone Town. For centuries, Stone Town had been a leading shipping port and market in the slave trade – a market conducted for the most part by Omani Arabs. In the 1800s, roughly fifty thousand slaves a year were brought by ships to the island's port at Stone Town. Famed explorer and missionary, Dr. David Livingstone, estimated that eighty thousand captured Africans died each year before they even reached Zanzibar's Stone Town slave market.

In 1873, when slavery finally came to an end in Zanzibar, abolitionist celebration began in the form of construction. A beautiful Anglican cathedral was built upon the site of the old slave market, the altar being placed where the old whipping post once stood. On the grounds nearby, five sculpted, life-sized slave figures, chained and bound, would later emerge as if from an underground holding pit – much like the very one that used to exist nearby. This artwork was created as a somber memorial to the slaves who suffered and lost their lives there. Beautiful cathedrals and monumental works of art however, did little of themselves to minimize the hardships and social inequities of free Africans in post-slavery Zanzibar.

By the early 1960s, Zanzibar was a constitutional monarchy overseen by a Sultan who, with his large family and roughly fifty-thousand other Arabs, continued to hold a tight grip on the islands' wealth and political power. Stone Town was still the center of commerce and home to mostly lighter-skinned Arabs, Indians, and Persians, along with a relatively small handful of Britons, Americans, and Europeans. The island nation's African population was three times larger than all other ethnic groups combined. Even so, Africans were mostly held to lower income labor jobs with little opportunity for a good education or improving their quality of life. Divisions and tensions between these economic classes reached a brief boiling point in early 1961. In January of that year, Africans became suspicious of local election fraud, and civil order was momentarily disrupted. A small uprising led to the violent deaths of sixty-four Arabs, but little changed for Zanzibar's African population. The strong undercurrent of class tensions and resentment submerged again for a time.

Letters from Farookh's parents never mentioned this political trouble and violence while he was abroad at a boarding school. Even if they had been mentioned, Farookh would have been too young to understand or to be too concerned about such matters, as long as his family was safe. If Arabs were to be the primary target of future uprisings, the young Farookh might have taken some comfort in knowing his family was of Parsee descent – not the least bit Arabic.

By early 1963, Farookh returned from school to his small family in Zanzibar and saw no traces of political turmoil, nor any hints of potential insurgency on the horizon. If anything, politically-minded African locals were hopeful that an upcoming election in July, unlike the previous one in 1961, might result in an appropriately fair number of parliamentary seats for their party. That hope was not met. Despite winning fifty-four percent of the popular vote, the Afro-Shirazi party only gained thirteen of the thirty-one parliamentary government's seats. Shortly after, the predominantly Arab government further reduced the opposition's political power by dismissing all police officers of African mainland origin. Budget cuts were then imposed reducing medical, housing, and educational benefits in ways that adversely affected impoverished Africans.

The Afro-Shirazi party voiced its complaints, but this time, no uprisings or clashes resulted in violent deaths. In the six months that followed, the Africans remained curiously quiet while their centuries-long anger and frustration continued to foment. During that time, most non-Africans, like Farookh, continued to enjoy their clubs, their white sand beaches, and their bicycle trips across the island, happily oblivious to the fierce discontent growing around them.

In the pre-dawn hours of Sunday, January 12th, 1964, an incensed young radical named John Okello caught a police armory's sentry by surprise, wrestled away his rifle and impaled the guard with his own bayonet. The other guards were soon overcome by Okello's band of African insurgents who quickly grabbed the armory's cache of guns and ammunition. Instead of sticks, knives, and machetes, the eight-hundred rebels now had firearms for attacks on Zanzibar City's police posts, prison, airport, and its local radio station.

By early morning, many of the government buildings – located in the Stone Town sector where Farookh lived – were under control of the revolutionaries. Farookh's family heard gunshots all around them and, like their neighbors, stayed locked inside with curtains drawn, listening to the alarming reports from their living room radios. At seven a.m., John Okello's first broadcast shook the airwaves.

"It is time for imperialists to awaken and depart from Zanzibar!" he proclaimed. "There is no longer an imperialist government on this island. We are the freedom fighters! Arise, black men! Men of Africa, take up arms against all oppressors until we have our freedom!"

Okello's threats were directed mainly at the Sultanate and Arabs in general, along with a promise not to harm any Europeans and Asians. By sunrise, having already been alerted to the budding revolution, the Sultan escaped the island on his royal yacht, along with his large family and several government leaders.

Upon hearing a report that one local police commissioner refused to surrender his station to the rebels, John Okello reversed his earlier promise with another cold-blooded broadcast. "The time has come for the commissioner to surrender without further delay. If not, I will come there myself and see to it that my soldiers kill *all* imperialists. All of you. Even Asians and Europeans if necessary."

The commissioner eventually surrendered, but all non-Arabs listening to the radio felt that they too might soon become victims of the violent rebellion. Before long, some of the shooting had become reckless, and terror ensued. There was looting of homes and businesses. An unsuspecting Catholic family was massacred while on their way to church. Several Asians were seized from their homes and put into harsh detention camps outside the city. One police officer was mutilated with machetes, his severed head and body parts spread across the hood of his car as a warning to all. In the end, hundreds of Arab and Asian women would be savaged, and thousands of Arab men would be gunned down and slaughtered.

On that first day of the revolution, seventy Americans, including those from NASA's Mercury tracking station, sought refuge at a waterfront Stone Town building known as the English Club. Their presence at the club was known to the insurgents, but they were left unmolested while the rampant killing of Arabs continued all around them. By various means, diplomats from the U.S. consulate in Zanzibar communicated news of the revolution to their homeland and plans were made to rescue American refugees. A navy destroyer named the USS Manley was sent from nearby Kenya to aid in the evacuation. The ship departed from Kenya immediately but was only allowed to dock at Stone Town's harbor at noon the following day. Much later that Monday evening, after hours of political wrangling between the Manley's officers and the rebels, the American evacuees finally received permission to depart Zanzibar.

The trouble was, the Manley's crew didn't know where the American evacuees were located. Officers on the ship's bridge scoured Stone Town with binoculars, looking for any sign of their distressed compatriots. The Americans holed up at the English Club could hear the ship's transmissions on a small portable radio, but amidst all the communication gaps, violence, and uncertainties, they had no means of letting the ship's crew know their whereabouts.

The rooftop terrace of the English Club offered an unobstructed northeast view over the whole of Stone Town, clear to the USS Manley moored less than a mile away. Two Americans from the NASA station, one of them a retired navy officer, decided to give semaphore signaling a try. From the club's rooftop, they eventually caught the attention of the ship's bridge. They also caught the attention of a young Parsee looking out from his second story bedroom window a short distance away. Farookh recognized the younger of the two American men as Mr. Morritsen, Jim and Patricia's father. Were they alright? Were the Americans also victims of the violent rebellion going on outside? Would his friends be leaving the island soon? With the window's curtains opened a sliver and the lights off in his room, Farookh kept his eye on the English Club's rooftop terrace until the two men disappeared inside the building at sunset.

There is very little evening twilight in Zanzibar. As Monday's sky quickly gave way to darkness, The USS Manley dropped two of its smaller boats into the water to fetch the American evacuees beyond Stone Town's pointy westward tip. Farookh could hear the revving of approaching boat engines as their propellers churned through the peaceful waters. He could also see the glare of floodlights coming from the back of the English Club. What Farookh could not see were the first two groups of American women and children being loaded onto the boats. The boat motors roared loudly again as their human cargo was taken back around the point to the USS Manley.

There were sporadic bursts of gunfire in town and the sound of the boats arriving and departing once more. The floodlights continued to glare from the back of the English Club driving Farookh nearly mad with concern for his friends. Were they safe? Were they still in the area? Would he ever see them again? Farookh knotted bedsheets together for a rope and lowered himself out of the bedroom window into the dark, narrow alleyway. Peering carefully around every corner and listening for footsteps, voices, and gunshots, he made his way over to the English Club just as the rescue vessels arrived a third time.

Behind the building was a small crowd of Americans on the beach looking relieved over the continuing arrival of the rescue boats. Farookh scanned the group and was happily surprised to see Jim Morritsen still there, standing next to his father.

"Jim! It's me, Farookh! Are you alright?" he asked as he ran up to his friend.

"What are you doing here, Farookh?" asked Jim incredulously. "You're going to get yourself killed! Don't you know they're killing Arabs like crazy around here?"

"Well, it's a good thing I'm Parsee and not an Arab then, isn't it?" said Farookh in a semi-humorous tone, trying to ease the immediate tension.

"You think they could tell the difference in the dark? Oh, never mind! Why did you come all the way over here?"

"I live just a short distance away," said Farookh. "I came here to see you – to see if you and your family were alright. I saw your father up on the rooftop earlier and wondered if you might still be here."

"We're fine, but I'm afraid we can't stay in Zanzibar any longer," said Jim. "My mother and Patricia have gone already. We're all heading over to the harbor. There's a big U.S. Navy ship over there, and it's taking us to Dar es Salaam on the mainland tonight."

"And then what?" asked Farookh.

"From there I guess we'll be heading back to the States. There's some kind of revolution going on here, and the Africans have taken over the whole city – maybe all of the Zanzibar islands, from what I hear. Anyway, it's not safe here. Haven't you been listening to the radio?"

"Yes, it's terrifying," answered Farookh, "but our family is hopeful we'll come through this alright. My parents came to Zanzibar from India, but they're here as British nationals, with British passports and all. If things get bad, we can always leave Zanzibar and come back later when things settle down again."

"My dad says there's another ship arriving soon to pick up any British evacuees. It's called the *Rhye*, or something like that. Hopefully, you won't need to leave, but maybe you could hop on the Rhye if you needed to."

"Maybe I'll flag the ship down from my rooftop," Farookh laughed.

Jim reached into his pocket and pulled out a small concealed item. He pressed it into Farookh's palm. Farookh stared down into his hand in disbelief.

"What's this, Hoople?" he asked, calling Jim by his nickname.

"It's a Derringer single shot pistol, Freddie," said Jim, returning the gesture. "I'm giving it to you. You'll probably have more need for it than I will. It's easy. Let me show you how it works."

"Where did you get this?" asked Farookh, while Jim put a bullet in the pistol's chamber.

"My father got it from one of the other Americans at the Mercury station. We don't need a small pistol anymore, but you might. So, take it!" said Jim. "And here's a few more bullets, just in case."

"But, I–"

"I need to leave now, Freddie," said Jim. The boats were preparing to head back over to the harbor with their next load of evacuees.

"Take care, Hoople," said Farookh, putting the tiny Derringer pistol into his own front pocket. He leaned forward to embrace his American friend.

"You too," said Jim. "Thanks for that great bike ride and for showing us around the island. It was a lot of fun!"

Farookh waved and watched as Jim headed down to the waterfront and stepped into one of the rescue boats.

"You'd better get out of here, young man," said Mr. Morritsen, approaching Farookh. "There's a small patrol of armed Africans coming up the beach. They're letting us Americans leave tonight, but it's not safe for you to be out here."

With that grim warning, Farookh quickly turned and headed toward his home. In his hurry, he missed clues of any unwanted company that might be lurking in the dim alleyways. As he rounded one corner, a hand violently shot out from a dark doorway and grabbed the front of Farookh's shirt. His body was whipped around and slammed hard against the building's plaster wall. An African rebel named Aboud pressed a machete against Farookh's throat.

"I've killed five people already today," the black man growled, "and I want to make it at least six."

"Please–" gasped Farookh.

"Don't you understand we are tired? We are tired of you running things and holding all the money and power while we break our backs for you and get nothing in return."

"I'm not–"

"I know who you are! Living in the lap of the gods, while our people hurt for fairness. I will not only kill you but your whole family as well!" The man pressed the blade tighter against Farookh's throat and moved it sideways, beginning to cut the skin. "Tomorrow, they'll find pieces of you in the street, and I'll know by who mourns the loudest who your family is!"

Just then, a light was switched on in an open third-story window nearby. Aboud was suddenly distracted and turned his view toward the window. In an instant of panic, Farookh saw both a chance to escape and a means to protect his family. He rapidly pulled Jim's small pistol from his pocket and raised it to Aboud's head. There was a loud pop, and for an instant, Aboud turned to look Farookh in the eye with a mixture of anger, disbelief, and fear before his knees gave way and his body collapsed onto the cobblestones.

Shivers went down Farookh's spine. With his heart pounding violently and his chest restricting breath, Farookh ran toward home pumping with adrenaline. He collapsed onto his bed and touched his neck to find drops of blood.

In the wide-awake hours that followed, Farookh relived the horror of that evening over and over until he finally gave in to exhaustion. The morning brought a new wave of terror as he awoke and remembered having killed a man the night before. Certainly, Farookh felt sorrow and remorse for the human life he had un-wantonly taken, but of far more significant concern was his family's safety. If Farookh were to be found and caught, he and his family would surely be put to violent death. If there were any sure hope of escaping this fate, Farookh imagined it could be only be found by leaving Zanzibar forever aboard the British ship, *Rhye*. Farookh continually fantasized about the ship's name and its travels through the Seven Seas as a distraction from his worries.

The third day of the revolution passed with Farookh's family still huddled inside their home. There were occasional gunshots and screaming heard outside. On the radio, John Okello continued to breathe threats of violence. So far though, there seemed to be no news about the dead rebel soldier in Stone Town, nor talk of any pending retaliation. Nervously, Farookh kept thinking of the man in the upper window who might yet identify him as the rebel soldier's killer. He anticipated insurgents breaking down the heavy wooden front door at any time.

Farookh was understandably startled by a knock on that ornately carved door the following morning. Eventually, he peeked outside his bedroom window and was relieved to see a friendly neighbor in the doorway below. "It's alright! It's Hoshie!" Farookh called down the stairs.

Once inside, Hoshie told Farookh's family about his plans to leave Zanzibar. "We can't stay here much longer," he said. "We have young children in our family, and they are starting to kill people by the thousands out there."

"But mostly Arabs. Isn't that so?" asked Farookh's father.

"Mostly Arabs, yes," said Hoshie, "but I hear a few Parsees have been killed as well. It's not safe here any longer. Even if we get to keep our lives, we'll lose our livelihoods. The Africans have taken over all the government and commerce offices."

"I see," said Farookh's father, with concern knotting his brow.

"A British navy ship has just arrived at the harbor. It's called the *Rhyl*," said Hoshie, using the ship's correct name. "It's departing in a day or two with all British citizens and nationals who want to leave."

"Where's it going?" asked Farook's father.

"To Dar es Salaam to begin with," said Hoshie. "From there, people are traveling to England, Canada, and Australia. I'm heading to Chicago myself. I have family there."

By that evening, Farookh could no longer contain the fearful emotions locked inside him. After sunset, when the sounds of gunfire had died down, he approached his mother who was sitting on a sofa. He kneeled on the floor and placed his head on her lap.

"Mama–" he cried.

"What is it Farookh? What's been bothering you so much these past days? We haven't been hurt by all this revolutionary nonsense going on."

"Mama ... I just–" sobbed Farookh, shaking and unable to finish his sentence. He couldn't make himself say the words and have his mother face the awful truth. She ran her fingers through his hair, offering comfort.

"Mama," he started again, "Hoshie's right. We've got to get out of here."

"And where do you think we should go?"

"To England!" said Freddie sitting up. "England's the place we ought to go!"

"Why there?" his mother asked.

"We have British passports. We can leave this all behind and start a new life there."

"Well then," said Farookh's mother, "I suppose now is a good time to tell you that we are planning to leave, perhaps as early as tomorrow or Friday. We're taking that British ship Hoshie spoke of, and we'll be heading for London."

"Really?!" asked Farookh. "Are we really going to London soon?"

"Yes, but it won't be easy," she said. "We can only bring a couple bags of belongings each, and England can get quite cold in the wintertime."

"I don't care, Mama," cried Farookh. "We've just got to get right out of here!"

That Friday, Farookh waited until the HMS Rhyl was well out to sea before he leaned over its side and quickly tossed the Derringer pistol and extra bullets overboard. He never looked toward the back of the ship to watch his homeland fade into the distance. He wouldn't have seen much of it anyway as tears of profound relief kept filling his eyes. Every mile between Farookh and Stone Town lessened the possibility that his friends and loved ones would be harmed for his killing of the rebel soldier. For this reason, he never contacted or acknowledged any of his youthful acquaintances ever again, and he never returned to Zanzibar, the land of his most tragic secret. Instead, Farookh would change his name, his appearance, and his lifestyle, hiding in plain sight as he transformed into a flamboyant, world-famous British rock musician. He and his family would be safe in England, a place where even police officers were said to carry no guns.

As for Aboud, he dwindled in darkness for a long, long time. It would be more than three Earth-centuries before he and Farookh would meet again.

Chapter 3: Rock of Ages

Our mortal bodies must be clothed with immortality.
Death, where is your sting? Grave, where is your victory?
The Apostle Paul

South of Damascus, Syria – 36 AD

"Saul," called a voice from directly above.

Saul lay flat on his back in the shallow, dark-orange dust of the old Damascus Road. Upon hearing his name, Saul tried to open his eyes, but they were pressed shut by a light brighter than the afternoon's desert sun. It seemed to come from the same direction as the voice.

Saul felt himself beginning to float up and away from the hot ground, or at least it seemed that way. Whether he was still in his physical body or outside of it at that point, he could not tell. The singular unfamiliarity of this supernatural experience filled him with both trepidation and amazement. The light increased its intensity as the voice called out again, "Saul. What is your business in Damascus?"

Saul was struck speechless, suddenly ashamed about the purpose of his travels. He and his zealous cohorts were on their way to Damascus to beat, arrest, and imprison members of a small but growing religious cult. The great crime of these apostates was their belief in a man who had died by crucifixion but reportedly came back to life days later by some miraculous means. Resurrection, they called it. Saul and his companions called it blasphemy.

"Saul. Why are you fighting against me? Why do you fight against goodness?" came the voice again.

"Who are you?" asked Saul, his eyes twitching and blinking as they began to adjust to the bright light.

"You know who I Am. I Am the Architect of the Resurrection," replied the voice, and with it began to appear its source – a radiant being standing before Saul. "Are you not familiar with the teachings of the prophets on this matter?" he asked. "Did not Daniel, Job, and Isaiah speak of the resurrection – the re-embodiment that follows mortality?"

Saul recognized his failure to comprehend those prophetic teachings with which he was quite familiar. The embarrassment left him unable to respond.

"What purpose," continued the glorious being, "do you see in the binding and whipping and jailing and stoning of people because of their belief in a physical life after death? Isn't that infliction of suffering an offense to your own spirit? Isn't it an offense to your own innate godliness? You are a child of God, are you not?"

Saul hung his head as he understood the error of his answer. "I thought I was doing God a service."

"Yes, I know, Saul. You are a good, sincere man, full of zeal and fervor," said the personage with a voice of compassion and understanding that moved Saul to trembling and tears. He became enveloped by increasing peace and comfort as the being stepped forward and took the quaking Saul into his arms. "There are better ways to direct that energy. I have another plan for you to follow."

Saul returned the embrace, holding on tight and sobbing for a long time over the countless, selfish errors he had made throughout his life, and the needless suffering he had brought upon others in recent years. When he finally stopped shaking, Saul humbly stammered out the words, "What would you have me do?"

"First," came the warm, kindhearted reply, "continue your trip to Damascus. You will be led to people there who will help you start a new phase in your life. It will not be easy, but you will have great opportunities for restitution and reconciliation. You will have a chance to help repair the damage caused to the people you have jailed and persecuted.

You will join them, become one of their apostolic teachers, and you will spread the word of resurrection's gift to all."

"Oh, thank you! Thank you! I'll do anything. I want to make things right!"

"I know you do, Saul. That's why I am entrusting you with this commission. If you can keep your eye single to this cause, throughout all kinds of trials and tribulations, even to the point of death, you may become a great teacher with influence upon the earth for centuries to come."

"I will serve with all my heart, might, mind and strength! You'll see!" Saul declared.

"Undoubtedly. But, first I would like to show you something. It will give you some perspective and understanding of our work – why we do all that we do. Watch this," he said with a broad sweep of his hand. In its wake was a wide swath of darkness, like the night sky.

"Abraham has seen this presentation before. So has Moses. And so why shouldn't you, Saul?"

The wave of darkness spread ever wider. In its center appeared an orb of mixed blues and whites.

"Do you see that, Saul? That sphere is the Earth. The world where you now reside – as seen from the heavens a great distance away."

A smaller, gray orb then appeared and began to circle the Earth.

"And now, what do you suppose that is?"

Saul was moved beyond speech and could not respond even as the answer formed on his tongue.

"It is the Moon, of course," the presentation continued, "The same light that rules the night sky."

Saul watched the Earth and the Moon became smaller as if they were quickly moving into the distance. Then a large, bright yellow sphere appeared. Beside it, the Earth seemed like a grain of sand.

"This is the Sun, the great light that rules the day and warms the sky and ground."

"Is it not the same size as the Moon?" asked Saul once he was able to gather his words together.

"It would appear so, yes, when you are standing upon Judea's plain. But in fact, the Sun is much larger than the Earth and the Moon, as you see here. The Sun is so much farther away from the Earth that it appears small in the sky. The Earth travels constantly around and around the Sun. Other worlds also join the Earth in these travels around the Sun. Perhaps you have seen some of them in the night sky. They are not stars at all, but the Earth's fellow travelers around the Sun. I will show you another star that is not a star. On a dark, moonless night you can sometimes see a bright, glowing speck in the sky. It is actually a cluster of many, many stars, all grouped tightly together."

"How many stars?" asked Saul.

"Countless. More than can be expressed by your Earthly language and understanding. But they are numbered to me, for they are mine."

"Are all the stars fellow travelers with the Earth also?" asked Saul.

"No. They are suns themselves, only they are so much farther away from the Earth that they look smaller. But I will show you that many of those distant stars are quite large indeed."

"Larger than the Sun?" asked Saul.

"Much larger, as you will see."

The panorama then showed the Sun being dwarfed by a parade of ever-increasing blue hypergiant and red supergiant suns that were then consumed by galaxies, galaxy superclusters, the universe, and multiverses. This imagery then slowly reversed its order ending with the planet Earth, where the vision drew closer and closer to ground level as seen from Saul's height.

"What are your thoughts at this moment, Saul?"

After a long pause, Saul answered, "I never realized it before, but mankind is no more than dust."

"'Nothing' is the word Moses used – 'Mankind is nothing,' he said. And how does this new understanding make you feel?"

"Humble," said Saul, "…and very small."

"That is fitting since you will eventually become better known on Earth by your Roman name, Paul. And Paul, as you know, means 'small.'"

"Many people called me 'Smalls' when I was a boy."

"I like the sound of 'Smalls' even better. I will call you by that name from now on."

"But," said the former Saul, "despite my size in the universe, something inside tells me I am greater than dust."

"Yes, Smalls. Regarding relative size, mankind may indeed be next to nothing – and yet, the worth of every person's soul is great. And many worlds throughout the universe are their hosts."

"Do you mean, there are people besides the ones on Earth?" asked Smalls.

"Yes. Great and infinite is our work and glory, to raise our children that they might rejoice with us in immortality and eternal life. And they, like the stars and other worlds in the heavens, are as numberless as the sands of the sea."

"All this … it's almost too much to comprehend," said Smalls.

"You have all of eternity ahead of you to learn and understand these things. For now, you need to know there are three stages to your existence."

"Three?" asked Smalls.

"Yes. The first stage was the life you enjoyed ages before you were born upon the Earth."

"I don't remember any of that. Not specifics anyway," said Smalls.

"It will all come back to you at some future point. In that first stage, it was decided when and where you would experience the very, very short, second stage of your existence. It is the one you are living in now, on Earth – your state of mortality. And when your earthly life comes to an end, you will enter Stage Three. It is a stage that goes on forever. It is the stage known as Eternity."

"What happens there?" asked Smalls.

"With Eternity comes the great gift of resurrection. You, along with all mortals, will regain your physical body in its prime and finest form, never again subject to illness, suffering, or death. It is a gift given freely to all – good or evil – who complete the second stage of their existence. And what will you do with these great gifts, Smalls?"

"I have never thought about it before," came the reply.

"With all your fervor and zeal in the service of God, you never thought of what you would do with your share of eternity? Here, listen to this."

Whether it was with his actual ears or just the comprehension of his mind, Smalls could not tell. He was only aware of a mesmerizing, pulsating, exotic sound not unlike the flow of Pink Floyd's *On the Run*. The music seemed to enter from all directions, gripping his soul and sending an electric tingling throughout his being.

"What do you think of that, Smalls?"

Several moments passed before Smalls could reply. "Wonderful!" he finally said with a fixed look of amazement and disbelief. "It's beautiful. And un-Earthly. I have never heard anything remotely like it."

"Ears have not heard, nor have eyes seen, neither have entered into the hearts and imaginations of mere mortals, the things which have been prepared for their reward."

"Music is one of the rewards?" asked Smalls.

"Music, art, poetry, dance, theater, architecture. Creativity of all sorts. New worlds without end. Yes, it is all part of that Stage Three reward that goes on and on forever."

"Forever? How can these things be?"

"Have you ever held flakes of snow in your hand, Smalls?"

"Yes, a few times. When I was young."

"Did you ever look at them closely? Did you ever notice their intricate patterns?"

"I have seen their many points and edges, yes," answered Smalls.

"Then I will tell you of another world called Deinousse. It is many times larger than your earthly home, Smalls. It has existed much longer than the Earth, and most of the time, in either the north or the south, it is snowing there. It has been snowing there for billennia. And I will tell you, Smalls, during all the storms and blizzards that have ever raged on Deinousse, no two identical snowflakes have ever existed there."

"That doesn't sound possible," said Smalls.

"And yet, it is true. And it is the same with music, which is far, far more complex than the patterns of snowflakes."

"What do you mean?" asked Smalls.

"Music is infinite, Smalls. One could compose music for eternity without duplicating a piece. Ever. Even when near matches do occur, they do so eons and eons apart. And thus it is that music fills eternity. Would you like to be a part of that musical eternity, Smalls?"

"I couldn't imagine anything greater!" came the reply.

"Then, after you have successfully completed your earthly mission, you will be rewarded with an even greater one. As a resurrected being, you will have responsibilities of collecting and preserving music from various and sundry worlds throughout the universe. You will have opportunities to help music be developed by struggling composers. You will see to it that music is collected, shared and expressed, taught and learned, performed and enjoyed throughout eternity. But first, you must return to *gethsemane*."

"Gethsemane?" asked Smalls. "Am I not to continue my journey north to Damascus?"

"Yes, but by *gethsemane*, I mean the winepress, or mortality, the second stage of your existence. It is the world of canine cannibals – dogs eating dogs, rats racing rats. Wars and rumors of wars. Survival of the greedy, selfish, and fearful. Of necessity, it is an extremely short phase of one's existence, for none could or should endure such horrors and suffering for long."

"If I might ask, then," inquired Smalls humbly, "why should anyone have to endure them at all?"

"It is unfortunate, Smalls, but the challenges and sufferings of mortality are for the good and experience of all people. Otherwise, most would remain dullards – no better off than the cows and goats. And I tell you, Smalls, Earth is one of the most difficult of all the gethsemanes. Gods and prophets have been murdered there as nowhere else. But instead of dullards, it is a world that brings forth musicians and artists and poets like no other. The more bitter the cup, the sweeter the song."

"I see," said Smalls.

"At this moment perhaps. But very shortly, your sight will be taken from you, as will the memory of much you have seen and heard this day. But remember, I am a rewarder of them that love me."

"Yes, Lord. I will love and serve you well. And I will be a great advocate of the gift of resurrection for all."

"I know you will, Smalls."

Moments later, the temporarily-blinded Smalls was helped off the dusty ground by his fellow travelers who had briefly heard a mysterious voice but had seen no bright light. Abandoning their original intentions for the trip, they continued their journey north to Damascus.

Chapter 4: Devils, Dullards, and Deities

Beautiful music is the art of the prophets ...
one of the most magnificent and delightful presents God has given us.
Martin Luther

Corcoran State Prison, California – November 2017

"You remember me?" asked the dying old man from his bed.

"How could I forget?" replied the visitor, almost concealing a slight chuckle as he spoke.

"No cameras?"

"No. You said no cameras, no crew, and no recorders. It's just the two of us here," replied the younger man, named Ron. "Looks like they're going to let us talk alone, as you requested." He nodded his head toward two infirmary guards who stood some distance away, inside the door but out of earshot.

"Dullards. Don't need 'em," said Charlie, quickly sticking his tongue out at the guards, crossing his eyes, and then squeezing them closed tight, wrinkling the crude, faded swastika tattoo between his eyebrows.

Same old Charles Manson, thought Ron Reagan as he considered the feeble skeleton before him. "So, what's this all about, Charlie?"

"Respect. It's about respect. That's why you're here. Not those other guys. They didn't show me respect like you did."

"You mean, that last TV interview we did? That was a long time ago."

"Yeah, and I'm on my way out now. I don't fear it. Love. Love is the opposite of fear. And all I have is love."

Ron had heard this spiel from Charlie before. He wasn't taking it any more seriously now than he had in the past, even though the old convict appeared to be on his deathbed. Whatever evil or mental disorder possessed the old man, he seemed likely as ever to carry it to his grave.

"Look, I know I've fed you some crap before. I was messed up. The Sixties, man! The four horsemen. *Helter Skelter*. Forget all that! It all added up to nothing," Charlie went on. "But this time is different. I've heard Eljay calling me."

"Eljay?"

"Him. You know. *Him* – with a capital *H*. You know the ancient written Hebrew had no vowels? That's what made his written name unspeakable. But in English, you can say it with all five vowels – no consonants – I-A-O-U-E, like that."

"Really," said Ron flatly.

"I understand He goes by Eljay nowadays. I've heard Eljay calling me back. I don't have much time left. I need to tell someone these things."

"What things?" asked Ron, trying to guide the conversation toward its point – if there was one.

"You're the only one. The only one who showed me respect. You gotta understand who I am. Who you are. Before I go. You gotta understand who we are."

"I know who you are."

"You know the name. You know the titles. You know the history. But you gotta see the big picture, man. Cinemascope! Technicolor! Smellavision! It's all there if you got eyes to see and ears to hear – like He says."

"So, what's the big picture?" asked Ron, an avowed atheist who wasn't buying any theological garbage from Charles Manson, of all people.

"Salt of the earth. Sprinkled like salt," said Charlie, starting to become surprisingly animated as he spoke. "Just one or two here and there. Billions and billions – dullards – most all of them. No better off than the cows and goats. But the salt's sprinkled on 'em. They're here. Just one or two here and there."

"Who?"

"God's children. The angels. The prophets. They have the knowledge. They have the power. They're the ones walking on water, healing the sick, raising the dead. I know. I met an angel once."

"Really? What was his name?" asked Ron dubiously.

"He said his name was Smalls. I didn't know he was an angel back then."

"An angel – named Smalls?"

"Yeah. Nice guy. He knew all kinds of interesting stuff about music. But the angels and the prophets – they're part of the yeast – the leaven. They're *raising* the dead instead of raising the bread. Don't you see?"

Ron was starting to get a little bored and impatient with this nonsensical conversation. He had come to the penitentiary in answer to Charlie's handwritten request – a matter of simple courtesy to one who had undoubtedly reached his last days. Ron also had to admit a bit of morbid curiosity had brought him here, not to mention a potential chance for historical notoriety. He felt he could likely be the last person to interview Charles Manson. And who knew? Maybe this time Charlie would have something new to say, perhaps something remorseful or even repentant for having incited those gruesome murders years ago. A full-blown deathbed confession perhaps. Instead, he found the old man rattling away with his usual drivel. Ron decided to humor Charlie with a few more minutes of feigned interest before excusing himself.

"I've never actually seen anyone walk on water," Ron mused.

"Your eyes aren't opened yet. You should see it. There are gods and angels and prophets all over the place. And devils. A lot more of them, but they are God's children too."

"Wait a second. So, who are God's children? I mean, first off, isn't everybody supposed to be God's children?"

"We were all there in the beginning," said Charlie. "All of us. In the beginning, there was light. We are light. When atoms split apart, there is light. All of us. All of Eljay's children. Even the Son of the Morning – the Morning Star – Lucifer, the Light-bringer. Most don't know anything about all this. But angels, prophets, gods, and devils are like salt – sprinkled here and there. Most of the mortal prophets are already awake and alive when they get here. And now they're trying to wake up everyone else. But the dullards won't listen. They won't see. Most of them anyway. The children of apes and frogs and swamps and lightning. And all that's true, but it's also a lie. 'A lie you got to rise above.'"

"But wait, so you're saying everyone is a child of God, but not really until they know it?"

"You're starting to see it now."

"So, all they have to do is know they are God's children to become God's children?"

"Knowing is just the start. There's believing. There's learning. There's following. There's becoming."

"But then, who are the devils?"

"They're salt too. Sprinkled here and there. There's not too much difference between a god and a devil. They have the same kinds of knowledge and power. The difference is how they use it."

"And so how do you tell who's a god and who's a devil?"

"The book says devils have a form of godliness, but they seek their own power. Their own law. Their own choices! Freedom, man!"

"Freedom?" asked Ron, internally enjoying the profound irony of the moment. "Charlie, how long have you been locked up here?" he asked wryly.

"It's the dullards' world, man. Way too many of them. Too much power. Strength in numbers. They don't understand. They don't know who I am. They're fearful. No love. Love casts out fear. And that's why they've kept me here. They're afraid of me. They're afraid – of nothing. Nothing to be afraid of."

After a pause to catch his labored breath, Charlie quietly added, "I had the power once. One of my songs even made it on a Beach Boys record. Did you know that?" Charlie began to hum an old melody to himself.

"And when you say prophets," interrupted Ron, "you mean like Moses?"

"Yeah, yeah. But there's more to it than that. You gotta see the big picture. Moses is like a law-and-order prophet. There are all kinds. There are architect prophets, carpet-layer prophets, doctor prophets, toilet-cleaner prophets, artist prophets. All doing their jobs right. All inspired. All inspiring. Sometimes folks will see and listen. The best prophets are the music prophets. All inspired. All inspiring. Sometimes they're the only ones folks will listen to."

"Who are they? The music prophets, I mean."

"I can't tell you their names. You have to see it for yourself. Hear it for yourself. Your ears are all closed up. But I'll tell you one thing. That young kid, John Mayer? You know him?"

"Yeah. I mean, I've heard a couple of his tunes on the radio," said Ron.

"He starts to see the big picture. He goes straight to the top in the music world all of a sudden. Soon he's got all the money and knowledge and power and women he wants. You heard his first hit? The one about him running through the halls of his high school? Listen to what he says. He's got it, man! His eyes are starting to open! And so, in the song, he's telling everybody about it! About how blind folks are. About what he sees – what he sees past all the lies. But hardly no one will listen. That's how it goes most of the time."

"John Mayer, huh? Is he a god or a devil?"

"All depends on what he does with himself, with his knowledge and power ... I don't know what became of him."

"Why are you telling me all this?" asked Ron.

"I got a chance, maybe. I got one last chance to make some things right. I'm trying to help you see things. Because you had respect."

"What – you get brownie points with your god or something if you tell me these things?"

"I don't know. All I know is that there's a chance. A chance to maybe make things right. To do something right. I had the power once. It's gone now."

"So, what are you, Charlie? A god or a devil?" asked Ron almost whimsically.

Once again, Charlie stuck out his tongue, crossed his eyes and then squeezed them closed tight, wrinkling the crude, faded swastika tattoo between his eyebrows.

"What do you think?"

Chapter 5: What Is and What Shall Never Be

*God makes the sun rise on the evil and the good,
and sends down rain upon the just and the unjust.*
Jesus

"What *is* this?" asked Giselle, suddenly sitting up straight, her ears taking in every note and nuance. "It's beautiful!"

"*Prad Lethnes Ot Esshen*," Smalls replied, speaking in Giselle's native tongue, a language from a distant world known as Deinousse.

Giselle knew this music wasn't from her home world, so she mentally struggled for a moment to guess its source and hopefully translate Small's response back into its original wording.

"*The Rain Song*," she finally breathed out with a slight hint of uncertainty.

"Quite right," said Smalls. "Your English is getting very good."

"So, it *is* from Earth then. What period?" she asked. "I've never heard anything like this before!"

"Eye hath not seen, nor ear heard…," Smalls muttered, mostly to himself, borrowing a phrase he had written in a letter to some friends long ago. His eyes seemed to gaze at a distant time and place while the music's Mellotron-synthesized strings provided background to his memories.

"It's modern, but doesn't sound like the 1960s," said Giselle, interrupting Smalls' distracted thoughts. "At least not the earlier Sixties stuff you've played for me."

"Yes, it's quite contemporary. Just a few Earth-years old, really," said Smalls. "It's from Earth-year 1973. This is turning out to be one of the greatest eras of composition this galaxy has ever produced. And it's still unfolding right now.

It's a little raw and rough around the edges, but that's part of what gives this music its energy and beauty."

Giselle was the most recent of protégés to be taught and trained by Smalls. Among his trainees were those who would occasionally provide help and inspiration to mortal composers. They were often referred to as angels, while those composers who heard the angelic inspiration and acted upon it were sometimes called prophets.

Giselle silently listened until the tune finished with a loud waterfall's rush of applause. There must have been thousands of audience members present when the performance was recorded, and their sound, together with the music, had given Giselle chills. "So, who were they – these *Rain Song* musicians?" she asked.

"Oh, they're still around," said Smalls as he lifted the needle from the shiny black vinyl disc. "The band's name is Led Zeppelin. Sorry, there really isn't a translation for that in your language, but they are from Great Britain."

"Yes, I thought it might be England. Or, maybe Canada," she said.

"This is the live version by the way, as you can tell by the appreciative crowd noise at the end. The studio version was recorded over five Earth-years ago."

"When you said they're still around – you mean they're still recording and performing?"

"Right now, actually," said Smalls. "In fact, they're just starting a show in a place called Oakland, California. I understand there are about fifty-thousand people there."

"Fifty-thousand people! I would love to be there, to see what that's like and to hear that sound performed. Could we go, Smalls?"

"Well, I'm not sure that's something we can ... It's just not part of our responsibilities right now, Giselle. Our job is to–"

"Please, Smalls!" begged Giselle. "There has to be some way to–"

"Patience, patience. You'll have plenty of opportunities to see them in the future – in our realm, of course."

"But that could take eons, Smalls. I want to see the origins and development of this music while it's happening. You said this was one of the greatest composition eras ever. Can't we watch it blossom in person, just for a few earthly hours?"

"Giselle, rare exceptions *are* made on occasion, but these things take time. You can't jump back into a Stage Two atmosphere all of a sudden. It's just not an environment you can transition to at a moment's notice – especially someone from such a gentle world like Deinousse."

"Please. Please, Smalls! You told me once that these eras don't last long – that they can suddenly change direction and vanish. I just want to capture this moment in history, while it's happening. I want to see this *Rain Song* band before they fade from their mortal fame and productivity. Smalls, I just want to–"

"Alright, Giselle. I'll see what I can do."

"Oh, thank you! Thank you, Smalls!"

"But it won't be today's show."

"Oh, but it would be so incredible to see that crowd of fifty thousand!"

"No, not today's show, Giselle. The only reason we might be able to do this at all is, you are right. There might not be much time left to see Led Zeppelin on Earth with a crowd this size."

"What makes you say that?"

"I have some inside information. Friends in high places, you know. I can't say too much about it, but right now in England, there's a young boy named Karac. He's on the verge of a serious illness. If things get worse for him, the odds increase that Led Zeppelin will soon experience its Flight of Icarus," said Smalls.

"Its what?"

"Its swan song, my dear Giselle – the ending of the band's compositions and performances in their mortal life."

"So, then, when would we be able to see them perform?" she asked.

"Not we, Giselle. Just you. I might be able to get you there, but you'll have to attend their next performance by yourself."

"But, when?"

"Well, tomorrow they have another show in Oakland, with much the same crowd size as today."

"Really?" exclaimed Giselle, clapping her hands together. "Oh, that would be wonderful!"

"I hope so," said Smalls, "but you might not find it as wonderful as you think. Earth isn't always as kind and peaceful as the world you lived on. Come along now. We have lots of preparations to make before sending you there."

******

Oakland, California – July 24, 1977

Smalls managed to round up the least conspicuous of cars, an older, dusky-blue Dodge Dart, to drive downhill toward the stadium.

"I haven't been back to Earth for nearly ten years. It turned out to be an unfortunate experience last time. I had to deal with a young composer named Manson – right here in California. He had some potential but was headed in the wrong direction. Made a huge mess of things," he said to Giselle with a sigh.

"Earth was your Stage Two home, wasn't it?" she responded, taking in the surroundings with wide eyes and a firm grip on the door handle.

"Yes, but that was a long time ago – on the other side of this world. Alright, do you see that up ahead? Those are the two Coliseum buildings. One has a roof on it, the other is open to the sky. You want the open one – the stadium. That's where the concert will be held."

"How do I get in?"

"I don't know all the details. You'll have to figure out a lot of these things yourself. But I do know you will need a ticket to get into the show, and you will have to pay money to get a ticket."

"Money?"

"Yes. It's printed paper. They use it here as a medium of exchange. It's made up of units called dollars. I'll give you twenty dollars, and that should take care of you for the day. There should be lots of people outside the stadium selling tickets. They call them *scalpers* – folks who buy lots of extra concert tickets hoping all will be sold and gone. Then when other people want to get tickets to a show, they will sometimes pay scalpers many times their original value."

"That's awful," said Giselle, "No one would ever think of taking advantage of people like that in my homeworld."

"I suppose it is awful, in a way," replied Smalls, "but sometimes there's an upside to all this. For example, I happen to know that scalpers over-purchased tickets for this show."

"What do you mean?" asked Giselle.

"It means they are stuck with too many tickets no one wants," Smalls replied with a smile. "And when that happens, they will sometimes sell their tickets for a very low price just before showtime. In any case, the twenty dollars I'm giving you should cover everything."

As Smalls and Giselle approached the stadium in the old blue car, they could see a small crowd forming at the property's fenced perimeter.

"I'm going to drop you off here," said Smalls. "You just mix in with the crowd over there and follow along with them until you get inside the stadium for the show."

"Isn't this exciting?!" squealed Giselle, who had been dressed in jeans and a tie-dye top with beads to blend into the atmosphere. "Oh, I wish you could go with me, Smalls. Don't you want to see this show?"

"Of course, I do, but I can't. Not today," replied Smalls, "I've got to get back and take care of some other matters.

Anyway, we've got our collection of the band's vinyl recordings I can listen to. Plus, I've already seen the film."

"What do you mean?"

"Led Zeppelin made a film of their live concerts a few years ago. Maybe we can watch it together when you get back."

"That would be great, but I'm really looking forward to seeing this show today as it actually happens."

"You just be careful," said Smalls, handing the money to Giselle.

"Don't worry," she said, "it's not like I can get injured or killed or anything. Remember, I'm immortal too, you know."

"Yes, but there are more ways to be injured than just physically. How does that phrase go? You're a spiritual being, first and foremost. But today, you're likely to have a very human experience, one perhaps unlike any from your own mortal life," said Smalls, sounding fatherly in his concern for Giselle. "Earth can be a rough place sometimes," he went on. "It's nothing like your homeworld. You say people don't take advantage of each other on Deinousse? Well, gods and prophets have been murdered here on Earth if you can you believe that." His eyes drifted back to some distant, mournful memories.

"I'm sure I'll be fine," said Giselle as she got out of the car. "Thanks for putting all this together for me, Smalls. I really do appreciate it."

"I'll meet you right around here after the show," he said as she closed the door. Giselle gave him a big smile and a wave through the passenger window and then turned toward the growing crowd nearby. Smalls drove eastward, back up into the hills.

It was a little after nine. A crowd of nearly three hundred people had gathered around a locked, narrow gate along the tall, chain-link fence surrounding the stadium and its parking lot. The show wouldn't start for a couple more hours, but early arrivers were either anxiously looking to buy general admission tickets, eagerly wanting to get a good viewing spot near the front of the stage, or both.

Several individuals were milling around, waving pairs of tickets in the air.

"Are those people scalpers?" Giselle asked a young woman with a yellow headband.

"Yes," she said, "but don't go buying from them right now. They want thirty, forty dollars a ticket. Wait until we get inside the gate. As it gets closer to showtime, their prices will drop way down."

The crowd had fanned into a semi-circle just outside the gate. On the other side stood two security guards who looked bored and disinterested. They shuffled their feet back and forth as they quietly chatted between themselves. Suddenly, a full bottle of beer was tossed in a high arc over the fence, crashing near the feet of the guards. Foam and shards of glass sprayed all over the asphalt just past the gate. The guards immediately snapped to attention. One of them began speaking into a hand-held radio.

Giselle, accustomed for so long to the peacefulness of post-mortal life, was surprised to hear herself let out a gasp. The crowd, there at the stadium for music that day, not civil unrest, turned around with a loud collective moan of disdain, many of them pointing toward the culprit. A couple of police officers soon appeared on the crowd's side of the fence. Without incident, they carted off the bottle-throwing offender who had been quickly identified by those around him.

In further hope of a more peaceful, enjoyable experience for all, a young man took it upon himself to make a public service announcement about the potential peril ahead. With the help of friends, he was boosted up above the crowd. The two security guards inside the fence looked on with concern, suspecting another potential troublemaker.

"Hey guys, listen up!" the young man shouted to the throng. "If I can get your attention for a minute!" The crowd, having doubled in size by that point, respectfully quieted down, curious if nothing else about what he might have to say.

"The gate here is only this wide," he announced, holding the palms of his hands a few feet apart. Speaking with an authority that apparently stemmed from experience, he continued. "I know we're all excited to get in there and see the show, but when they unlock the gate in a few minutes, we're going to need to go through the gate nice and easy, or people are going to get hurt. Nice and easy, okay?"

The conscientious young man was lowered back down to ground level while the guards on the other side of the fence nodded their approval of his cautionary message. The concern was legitimate. About a month before, more than 160 panicked people were trampled to death at a show in Kentucky. Over a hundred spectators and police were injured at a Led Zeppelin concert in Florida just a few weeks earlier. And, two and a half years later, eleven attendees would be crushed to death by crowds at a Cincinnati rock concert featuring The Who. Giselle had no awareness of those facts and wondered about the need for such a warning. What could possibly go wrong? With the beer bottle hurler now long gone, the crowd seemed a perfect example of "nice and easy."

Close to ten o'clock, the security guards stepped forward to unlock the gate and then quickly stepped back from the oncoming stampede. As the gate swung open, jubilant teens ignored the earlier warning and began streaming through at full speed. Once past the gate, they broke into a full run, rushing to join the entrance lines forming closer to the stadium.

Giselle found herself moving nearer the gate, not so much of her own accord, but by the force of the crowd pressing in tightly all around her. She was like one grain of sand among many, all flowing downward toward the pinched center of an hourglass. Passing through the fence's narrow gate would not be nearly as smooth, however.

Soon there were cries of frustration, anger, and pain as some were pushed and pinned against the chain-link fence on both sides of the gate. Giselle could see she was involuntarily moving toward that same fate. As the crowd thoughtlessly pushed from behind, friends in trouble called and reached out to one another for assistance, but Giselle had no one. The security guards inside the perimeter just stood back and smiled, amused at the entertaining scene.

Forced against the chain-link fence, the side of Giselle's face was pressed into its diamond-shaped weave. The closest avenue of escape was through the gate, a few feet to the right. Gripping the fence, she inched that direction. As she got closer, she could see others popping through the gate at a steady, consistent rate – one every half second or so. But when Giselle reached that point herself, the constant popping stopped. The gateway had become clogged, and yet the crowd kept surging and pushing from behind in relentless waves.

The persistent force suddenly broke the logjam as Giselle and four or five others exploded through the gateway all at once. She lost her footing, tumbled to the asphalt, and rolled more than once through the broken beer bottle glass. Giselle came through unscathed but realized any of the mortals around her would have suffered severe cuts in that same situation. Still, the security guards standing nearby paid no attention to her plight. They continued to chuckle at the chaotic show playing out before them.

After getting back on her feet and regaining her bearings, Giselle ran to join the queue forming ahead. Once having secured her position near the front of the line, there was time to reflect on the harrowing experiences of the morning so far. Glancing around, she observed a general mixture of glee. People around her were laughing over having survived the gate ordeal and successfully arriving so close to the head of the entrance line.

"Maybe that's the kind of rough experience Smalls was trying to warn me about," she said to herself. "Maybe that's all there is." She began to relax again in anticipation of the music she came to hear.

Just then, the laughter around her suddenly got louder, directed at some spectacle a short distance away. A lone black Toyota sitting out in the middle of the parking lot was approached by a staggering young man. He collapsed onto the car's hood, embracing it while the crowd hooted and jeered.

"He's smashed already!" a guy with a long dark beard exclaimed. "Hey, it's a little early, isn't it?" he shouted in the direction of the Toyota. Everyone around, except for Giselle, responded with laughter. She couldn't detect any reason for the hilarity. The young man was apparently suffering from some kind of illness.

After a moment of rest, the inebriated fellow lifted himself from the car's hood, fumbled with his zipper and, with his back to the crowd, began to relieve himself on the front tire. Suddenly, he lost his balance, spun around mid-stream, and exposed himself to the howling masses. After another spinning stumble, he wrapped his arms around the car's trunk to steady himself and finish his business.

A few moments later, the young man staggered back a few steps and then lurched his upper body forward with three long blasts of clear vomit. Each time the crowd gave a roar of mixed disgust and delight. Giselle kept fighting the idea of going over to help the young man. She wasn't sure if he truly needed assistance though, as everyone around her seemed to find more humor than alarm in the situation.

"Do you have your tickets?" a no-nonsense voice suddenly and sharply demanded, distracting Giselle from the sad display nearby. She looked up to see a man with a hat, sunglasses, and an official-looking bright orange vest. Before she could reply, the man behind the shades continued to address Giselle and those around her. "We'll be coming back around in about ten minutes to check everyone's tickets. If you don't have one, you'll need to move back outside the fenced area. We'll be opening up the stadium gates in about a half hour, and we need everyone in line to have their tickets ready."

Looking around, Giselle could still see scalpers wandering the grounds, holding up tickets for sale. "Do you already have your ticket?" she asked the young woman with the yellow headband, who ended up at the same place in line.

"Yeah. If you don't have a ticket, now would be a good time to get one. I can hold your place here in line if you want."

Giselle nodded in thanks and quickly walked off. She was back a short time later with ticket in hand, having only paid twelve dollars for it. Giselle normally would have felt quite pleased with herself, speaking the local language on this foreign planet, and successfully negotiating her ticket purchase. But these successes did little to ease her general discomfort with the raucous, ungodly, human atmosphere in which she now found herself wholly immersed. She felt safest sticking near the young woman with the yellow headband, watching her for clues on how to navigate in this unfamiliar environment.

The line began to compress, moving forward in jolts as the anticipated time for the stadium opening drew near. When the gates opened, Giselle and all the other attendees were quickly subject to an uncomfortable search as the security team checked for prohibited alcoholic beverages and glass bottles. She had to force herself to raise her arms and allow her body to be patted down. She squeezed her eyes shut and numbed her mind as the unexpected frisking took place. When it was over, Giselle got caught in the next stream of fans charging toward the stage in hopes of seeing the band up close.

As Giselle's feet hurriedly moved along, her eyes became fixed upon the immense, colorful stage. It was decorated in the colossal imagery of Stonehenge and above it rose a giant model of a zeppelin, representing the day's headlining act. Beforehand, Giselle could never have imagined such a breathtaking sight. Finally, there was no more room for Giselle to run as the crowd compacted near the front of the stage. The early arrivals dropped down onto the grass field, staking their territorial claim while awaiting the start of the show. The stadium's sound system was blasting out a deafening, distorted stream of somber tunes that left Giselle feeling more depressed than uplifted. They sounded nothing like *The Rain Song*.

Curiously, a man sitting next to her began applying white coloring all over his face, then bright red to his lips before punctuating his eyes with dabs and outlines of black. He donned a tall hat, stood up, and began to ascend an invisible rope that seemed to rise high into the air. He swayed back and forth as he climbed further and further upward but never seemed to grow more distant. Giselle had to keep looking down at his feet to confirm they were still touching the ground. The illusion made her feel slightly disoriented and dizzy. She had never seen anything like a mime's performance before.

Nearby, another distraction was increasingly drawing attention. Almost a dozen people, all grabbing onto the edges of a large blanket, were repeatedly tossing a teenaged girl higher and higher into the air. There was a grin on her face, but her limbs waved frantically, hands and feet clawing at the air as she approached increasingly dangerous heights. Cheers from nearby observers rang out each time the girl shot up high into the air. Then there was a sudden unanimous moan when, by some mishap, she missed the center of the blanket, bounced off the ground, and began crying loudly with the pain of a dislocated shoulder. Friends helped the sobbing girl away from the stage and went to seek medical help. Giselle's eyes, full of pity and concern, followed the girl until she was out of sight.

The depressing loudspeaker music ended abruptly as a man stepped up to one of the microphones on stage. He welcomed the audience and made several echoing announcements about crowd safety and upcoming shows. As the man's address began, the concertgoers on the lawn rose to their feet at once. They started to press tightly up against the crowd barriers in front of the stage. Not having much choice, Giselle moved up with them. She was packed in tight.

Getting the day's show officially underway, the man at the microphone made a loud, enthusiastic announcement. "Ladies and gentlemen. Will you please welcome, from Birmingham, England – Judas Priest!"

The band's very name brought a sourness to Giselle's core for reasons she couldn't readily discern. She only knew the name didn't sound like Led Zeppelin. And neither did the music. The band quickly launched into *Call for the Priest,* with its driving rhythm guitar and drums pounding mercilessly against her eardrums.

Giselle had not been aware there would be other acts besides Led Zeppelin playing that day. Even if she had looked at her ticket earlier, it said nothing about any other bands. She was so squeezed in on all sides now that she couldn't have reached that ticket in her pocket just to check.

"Is this the Led Zeppelin concert?" she asked a bearded face right up next to hers.

"What?" he yelled back.

"Is this the Led Zeppelin concert?" she asked in a louder voice, hoping to be heard above the thunderous music this time. A few people around her began to chuckle in disbelief over the ridiculous question.

"Well, yeah," the bearded guy responded, joining in the laughter over her ignorance or confusion, "but they won't be on stage for a while yet!"

The sun broke through the morning mist and began beating down on the masses below. The music from Judas Priest was loud and distorted. The crowd near the front swayed and swelled like ocean waves. There was groping.

Giselle's eyes started to flutter. It was too much. Too much. The noise. The suffocation. The waft of humanity's lesser character. She struggled to turn around, to face away from the stage and, inch by inch, work her way toward an exit. She had to get out of there. There was no longer any enjoyment or excitement in this. No music, however beautiful, was worth the sensation of grime she could feel all over her skin. As she forced her way through the crowd, there was more pinching and grasping. With her eyes still fluttering and her breathing coming in short, high-pitched gasps, Giselle began to cry. None of the surrounding faces seemed sympathetic to her dilemma. Some began laughing at her distress and her struggle to get through the crowd, just as they had laughed earlier at the guy vomiting out in the parking lot. Giselle felt a little like puking herself.

Suddenly, the press of the crowd loosened around her. Giselle could feel a comforting arm encircle her shoulders. She looked up with her watery eyes but could see little else but the blinding light of the sun. It made her wince. Her guide's smooth, calming voice said, "Come on. We're going to get you to a safer place."

The sea of people now parted easily before them and Giselle's crying soon ebbed. Wiping her eyes, she looked up again and saw her savior's long hair flowing behind him, bouncing lightly with every stride.

With a gentle smile, he looked at her and said, "I'm guessing you've had enough excitement for one day."

"Yes," she admitted, with surprise that he should know exactly what she was thinking and feeling. "It was a little more than I was ready for. I thought I could handle it."

"'Upon us all, a little rain must fall.' Isn't that right?" the kind man replied, "But I'm sure you'll get plenty of other chances to see shows like this."

"Maybe," she said doubtfully. "I'm starting to think vinyl records are probably the best way to enjoy some kinds of music."

"Oh, I don't know," said the man. "I had some bad concert experiences at first too, but I eventually found ways to enjoy them. I go to as many of the good ones as I can. You see that uncrowded spot way up there in the stands? That's where I'm sitting. No pushing and shoving up there."

"You're going to stay for the rest of the concert?" asked Giselle.

"Wouldn't miss it. I don't care that much for Judas Priest, but Rick Derringer's band is going to be on stage in a while. Fun show. Lots of energy. Besides, this might just be Led Zeppelin's last performance in this part of the world."

Giselle quickly turned her head toward the man's face, trying to discern how he might have possessed even the slightest such notion.

"Anyway, here we are," he said as they neared the stadium's exit. "That's your ride, isn't it?"

Giselle looked out past the stadium's parking lot and its chain link fence. There was Smalls, waving to her from the dusky-blue Dodge Dart across the street.

"How did you know?" she asked, turning again to the long-haired man. But he was gone.

Chapter 6: Dregs of the Earth

Now let the band play Dixie*; it belongs*
neither to the South, nor to the North, but to us all.
Abraham Lincoln

"And, if I could get a side order of grits too please, that would be great."

"Oh, you bet. I'll be back soon with your order," said our server as she turned, heading back toward the kitchen.

"Lawrence, what did you just ask for?" asked my new bride, Cheryl.

"Grits," I responded.

Cheryl paused for a moment. "Isn't that something the *Beverly Hillbillies* eat?"

"Could be," I said. "I'm not really sure."

Cheryl was intrigued by my last-minute decision to order grits at an all-day-breakfast cafe in San Jose. I suppose she had good reason. She had never seen me order grits before. It was the first time for me too.

"Well," she started, then paused for a moment. "What are they?"

"Grits, you mean? I guess we'll find out when they get here."

"So, you ordered grits, and you don't even know what they are?"

"Yeah, I just saw 'em there on the menu and thought I'd give 'em a try. What could go wrong?" I asked. "I mean unless they end up tasting like anchovies or something."

There were several unfamiliar menu items I could have ordered that day and Cheryl would have been equally curious about any of them. But she wouldn't have understood the real reason why I ordered grits that morning, so I never offered any explanation.

"And there's your grits," said our server after she had placed the rest of our breakfast items on the table.

I stared deep into the small bowl, trying to discover its mysteries. Cheryl sat up straight to get a better view as well. There wasn't much to look at, just a thick white mush that solidly held its flat surface level with the bowl's rim.

"What's it like?" asked Cheryl, after I touched a spoonful to the tip of my tongue.

"Well, it's hot," I replied, "but the flavor's sort of bland. Not in a bad way, though. I mean, it's kind of like rice or mashed potatoes that way. Wanna try some?"

I wondered if I was doing it right. Was I supposed to put something on the grits, like salt, or pepper, or Tabasco sauce? I had no idea. Since the grits resembled oatmeal somewhat, I did something that would probably make many Southerners shake their heads and wince. I decided to fuse Yankee North and Deep South by sweetening those grits with maple syrup. I then dug into them with the subconscious hope of developing a closer bond or kinship with my favorite band of all times, the Dixie Dregs. A friend of mine had once misinformed me about the band's original name, telling me it was the Dixie Grits. When I saw to my surprise that grits were available at that San Jose restaurant, I knew I had to try some.

I cried when I heard that Dixie Dregs guitarist, Steve Morse, had died. I cried on and off for several hours. I skipped work that day. I called in sick. No way was I going to work with my nose all red and my eyelids all swollen. And for what? What would I have said? Who would have understood? Absolutely no one – not even Cheryl. I wasn't sure if even I comprehended this sudden emotional outpouring and I needed some time to process it all. I coughed a bit over the phone when I told the boss I wasn't coming in.

"Yeah, you sound a little under the weather," he said, noting the slight hoarseness, however affected, in my voice. "Hope you feel better soon. We'll see you maybe tomorrow."

I never met Steve Morse, but as a founder of the Dixie Dregs, he had been a significant part of my mortal life for over half a century – ever since that time KSAN radio played one of their tunes. I never heard it played on the radio ever again. In fact, I only ever heard Dixie Dregs music played over the airwaves maybe two or three more times in the following decades. But on that first occasion, at age seventeen, I stood fixed and still after drawing up close to the radio. I turned the volume up and listened and waited. There were no vocals. No lyrics. Just music. Pure music.

What is this stuff? Who are these guys? I needed to know. But when the tune was over, the radio station cut straight to a car dealership commercial.

I stretched the coiled white telephone cord far from the wall as I flipped back and forth through the phone book's yellow pages on the kitchen counter. Real Estate. Radiators. There ... Radio Stations and Broadcasting Companies. I punched the numbers for KSAN into the handset, grateful that my parents had finally replaced the old rotary dial phone with a new push-button model. I kept getting busy signals before I finally got through.

"KSAN 94.9, San Francisco. How can I help you?" answered a voice on the other end of the line.

"Hi. What was that music you guys just played?"

"You mean, before the station break?"

"Just before the car lot commercial, yes. There was no singing – just a band playing music," I added.

"Let's see ... That was the Dixie Dregs. The tune's called *Take It Off the Top*. Nice stuff, huh?"

"Yeah, it was great! Are they a new band?"

"I'm not sure, but it looks like the album is brand new. We just got our promo copy yesterday."

"What's it called?"

"*What If.*"

"What??"

"*What If.* That's the name of the album."

Less than thirty minutes after that brief phone conversation I was pedaling my bike back home from the nearest record store with a vinyl copy of *What If* hanging from my handlebars in a white plastic bag.

I raced inside the house knowing no one else would be home for at least another hour and I planted that LP on my parents' stereo console. Cranking up the volume, I lowered the needle onto the second track, purposely skipping *Take It Off the Top* to sample the rest of the album. The next tune was *Odyssey*, another roller coaster instrumental loaded with a bunch of tricky time signature changes – a challenge readily met by the band's virtuosity. In fact, the whole album was nothing but intellectually stimulating instrumentals.

I became an instant fan. I felt like it was *my* music – like I was born into this particular time and place so I could experience Dixie Dregs tunes during my lifetime. Had I been born a century earlier, I know I would have walked through life forever unsatisfied, longing and thirsting and yearning for music that did not yet exist. And I know that many Earth-centuries from now, the timeless nature of this music will still be around, and it will still sound good to any great-great-grandchildren of mine who might take a listen.

For a Bay Area kid like me, it never felt better or happier to be an American than when I listened to Dixie Dregs music. And I mean "American" in the best possible way – no hydrogen bombs, no Vietnam War, no Watergate, no Iran-Contra dealings. There was only pure, exultant joy in those rapid-fire notes played by Steve Morse on a tune called *The Great Spectacular*. Music like that does not come from Somalia, Uzbekistan, Paraguay, or even Britain or Canada. It is barely even heard in the United States, let alone Greenland, Tunisia or Singapore.

And yet it wasn't exactly an America I had a full, honest familiarity with. Steve Morse and the Dixie Dregs hailed from the South – the Deep South, as I had heard it called – and I had never set foot further south or east than Fresno when I first heard their music. But to me, it represented the very best of what I imagined the Southland to be – no slavery, no Confederacy, no fire hoses blasting marchers, no segregation. Instead, listening to *Gina Lola Breakdown* was like the heart-melting lilt in the voice of a young Mississippi housewife. It was tasty deep-fried foods. It was the famed Southern hospitality. It was sitting on the front porch after supper, talking with neighbors and folks strolling by. Listening to *Night Meets Light* reminded me that each and every day, as the Earth completes its rotation, the sun rises on us all, whether we are from the North or South. That music did not come from Chicago, Omaha, Boise or Seattle. It is distinctly American music even though it is barely even heard in Duluth, Buffalo, Winnemucca or Barstow.

And that's why I started eating grits, I suppose – trying to make a better connection with this distant, unfamiliar Southland where the music of the Dixie Dregs was born. Trying to make a better connection with whatever I felt was good about my home country. Trying to find and feel the very best of America inside myself.

When the Dixie Dregs announced their 45th-year reunion tour, people from places as unlikely as Duluth, Buffalo, Winnemucca and Barstow all begged the band to come to their little towns. The thought that the Dixie Dregs would ever come to a place as remote as Eureka, California, where Cheryl and I lived, was so far from reality that it never crossed my mind to make such a request. Instead, I hopped a plane across the entire country to see one of their opening shows in Augusta, Georgia. It wasn't like I hadn't done some traveling to see the band before. On at least two occasions I had raced through mountain passes in my little compact car just as the highway patrol officers were starting to require tire chains in oncoming blizzard conditions. I had no chains, but I wouldn't let that fact, or anything else, get in the way of seeing a rare Dixie Dregs concert.

Their music was soothing to me in times of stress or sorrow. It kept me company when no one else was around. There were no better travel tunes for cruising the back roads.

And even without any audio equipment, I could always hear those tunes clearly in my head when I wanted to. They were like the soundtrack to my life.

Even so, Dixie Dregs fandom was a lonely life for me. Curiously, not many friends shared my appreciation for this obscure band. In fact, in all my earthly years I only met a small handful of people who had ever even heard of the Dixie Dregs, let alone liked them. In all this time, even Cheryl doesn't fully understand.

And then when Steve Morse died – the one who united and held that fivesome together since the very beginning – the world suddenly got all the lonelier. There would never be another new album. There would never again be another reunion tour. When Steve Morse died, the Dixie Dregs naturally came to an end, and part of my soul went with it.

But I still listen to the *What If* album now and then. And for the longest time, I have eaten grits with maple syrup.

Chapter 7: Giant Silence

[Heaven] ... where there is only life
and therefore all that is not music is silence.
George MacDonald

Rogue Valley, Oregon – July 2006

During the minister's closing remarks came the bleating of a neighbor's goat, making all the wedding guests chortle. The minister smiled along with them. Behind thick-rimmed glasses, the corners of his eyes wrinkled with the delightful moment of humor.

Before long, the outdoor ceremony came to an end on that warm summer evening, and the guests grouped themselves together at tables with fancy centerpieces. The estate sloped upward on its west side, reaching into nearby hills of scrub oak, madrone, and evergreen trees. Behind those hills, the evening sun had dropped, and the sky darkened from blue to a deep purple. Venus and several stars made their early appearance.

A hired local band began to play on a warmly lit patio near the house. They called themselves Giant Silence and their music might have been best described as spirited, but suave and sophisticated. It had a subtle, imperceptible way of stirring the soul.

If you had asked the band's frontman, Antone Westgate, he would have conceded that Giant Silence was never headed for stardom, never meant to headline a show, or to have a hit single. For seven years, Giant Silence had been playing clubs, lounges, and wedding receptions in the valley, and that's right where they were meant to be. The bride's family, on whose ample property the outdoor wedding took place, knew little of such things. They were just grateful when a thoughtful family friend recommended Giant Silence for the reception.

Subconsciously absorbing the beautiful patio lights and surroundings, the wedding guests chatted away while dining on salad, colorful pasta, and chicken parmesan. All the while an undercurrent of music was welling, barely noticed below the friendly chatter and all the attention drawn to the newly-married couple. Only three or four appreciative guests seated near the patio offered low, polite applause as Giant Silence's first few tunes came to an end. Each time, the solidly-built Antone, wearing a classy black tux and top hat, smiled and softly said, "Thank you," into the microphone.

Without introduction, the band's next tune got underway. Two backup singers draped in long black silky gowns gently swayed with the rhythm of the stick tapping on the snare drum's rim and the smooth shaking of the maraca. Light saxophone, guitar, and keyboard joined in, and Antone began a hardly noticeable stepping back and forth, microphone in hand. His shoulders raised and dropped a little with the beat and his face moved side to side, left to right, left to right. Bit by bit, the tune was building up energy, being born into a life of its own.

Giant Silence had comfortably locked itself into a tight groove, one that, like an octopus, softly began to reach out and wrap its tentacled arms around the souls of those with ears to hear. Even for those not paying attention to the music, conversation dropped in volume and feet began gently tapping beneath the tables.

It was moving. The music was moving. Moving along and enlarging itself and feeding off its own energy. Antone began a low, rhythmic chant into the microphone, expressing gratitude and joy for the music and its rare magic on this occasion. He was a sorcerer, recognizing the scarcity of such moments in life, working that groove, that pulsating groove, tighter and tighter, louder and louder. The band, the audience, the surroundings were all suddenly joined together, seemingly lifting off the earth's face, removing to a higher plane.

"Excuse me. Could I–"

The bride's father suddenly stepped up close to Antone and reached out to grab the microphone. Antone's smooth voice was cut off, and it took a couple more moments for the band to realize what was happening before they too – in perfect fulfillment of their name – stopped playing.

The beaming father was giddy over the marriage of his daughter and dutifully oblivious to the sublime, mesmerizing swell of the band's spontaneous, heavenly flight. Into the microphone, he blurted, "Thank you all for being here this evening. If I could just have your attention for a moment, I'd like to propose a toast to the newlyweds!"

Sometime later, the hired band went back to doing their job that evening. And that's what Giant Silence sounded like – merely a hired band. When the gig was over, they put instruments back into their cases and went home. The band's musical soul had been beaten and bruised like this one too many times and Giant Silence never re-grouped after that. The transcendental moment was lost and forgotten. Where it might have gone would never be known, and no force in the universe could ever again rekindle it.

Chapter 8: Karac and Giselle

I may be old, but I got to see all the cool bands.
Early 21st Century Bumper Sticker

Eureka, California – March 2030

As my eyes opened, I could tell I was in some kind of large container, surrounded by metal railings and racks – aluminum mostly. Kneeling next to me was a man with dark hair and glasses. He asked if I could tell him my name.

"Sure," I said, "It's Lawrence. What's yours?"

Another person nearby was going through my wallet, but in a dazed state of mind, I didn't mind in the least. The name I had given them was confirmed by my driver's license, and the two gave each other a nod of affirmation.

"My name's Bruce," the kneeling man replied. "Don't worry. We're gonna take good care of you." I slowly grasped that I needed 'good care' for some reason.

"What happened?" I eventually asked.

"There was an accident," said Bruce. "But we're gonna take good care of you."

"Where's Eric?"

"Don't worry about Eric. We're taking good care of him too."

Reassured, I closed my eyes again. I never felt the forward rolling motion of the ambulance or heard its siren along the way to the hospital.

A short time later, I felt my body being jostled. I opened my eyes and saw the man with the dark hair and glasses again as he finished his hospital delivery. With a sudden realization of appreciation for his help, I managed to recall his name and said, "Thanks, Bruce."

He gave me a nod and a smile. "Take good care," he said. As I was wheeled away, my eyes closed once again.

It's hard to say how much time lapsed. It felt like I had been gone for hours. Maybe longer. I felt rested and refreshed, but at the same time hazy as if waking from the long deep sleep of a long deep dream. Shapes around me started to become more and more distinct. I was sitting in the most comfortable of armchairs in a small, warmly-decorated room, with astoundingly beautiful, light-colored wood paneling.

"You made it. Welcome back," said a pleasant voice nearby. I became aware of a young man sitting across from me in the same type of armchair. He had all the appearance of a Norse god – long, full blond hair with a reddish tint and a short, slightly darker beard. He was wearing a silky robe of extraordinary whiteness. Even his very being seemed to have something of a glow or aura to it. I soon became aware that I was similarly dressed.

"Where am I? Is this the hospital?" I asked the young man.

"This is the Third Stage," he replied. "You're in the reception area. You made it!" I noticed that he spoke with a slight British clip. "Yes, there's the First Stage, the Second Stage and all that. It'll come back to you soon enough."

I paused to consider his words, but no memories were triggered. The last thing I recalled was thanking that Bruce guy after we arrived at the hospital.

"And where's Eric?" I asked. "Is he okay?" I felt sure Eric and I had been together whenever the accident supposedly occurred.

"Eric is just fine. Well, actually, his ribs are going to hurt for a while, and he'll have to sleep in a special bed for a few more months. But, not to worry! It won't be long, and everything will be right as rain with him."

I noticed that I felt just fine myself. Not just fine but light and free. I sensed life and vibrancy to an unimaginable degree. I had all the energy of a three-year-old but felt strangely content just to sit and converse with this pleasant blond being before me.

"So, what happened?" I asked.

"With you and Eric, you mean?"

I nodded.

"There was an accident."

"Bruce said that – the guy in the ambulance with me."

"Oh yeah. Bruce is a good chap. He helps a lot of people. Anyway, your car was in the shop, so you asked Eric if you could catch a lift to work with him. You guys stopped at a red light, first in line, and when the light turned green, you started to go. Unfortunately, a lorry driver – I mean, a truck driver – ran the red light from the other direction and smacked his semi right into Eric's driver side."

"And he's okay, you say?"

"Eric, you mean? Oh yeah, he'll be just fine. But you know Bob Sellers, who lives on your street? Well, he's an insurance adjuster, and he took one look at Eric's pickup over at the wrecking yard and said, 'No one should have survived that accident.' Want to see the picture he took?"

Before I could answer, the young man spread his hands out before me. Between them appeared an image of Eric's pickup truck in the junkyard. All the windows were shattered, and the frame was twisted like a DNA helix. The driver's side of the cab was smashed in.

I felt sorry for Eric with his rib pains and all but had to marvel at how exuberant I was feeling after being in such an awful wreck. It seemed nothing short of miraculous.

"Where did you say this place is, again?" I asked.

"Well, this is the Third Stage reception area, and I'm here to welcome you. Karac's my name, and you were called Lawrence, right? Folks who knew you back in the Second Stage will probably always call you Lawrence."

"I don't know anything about all these stages," I interrupted. "How many are there?"

"Just three, basically," said Karac. "A lot of things seem to come in threes around here. You'll start recalling all of this soon enough."

"So, where is *here*?" I asked. "And is Cheryl alright? What about the kids?" Karac was right. Memories were starting to return. It was like coming around again after general anesthesia.

"Don't worry. They're just fine. They'll be well taken care of, as always, and you'll see them all soon enough."

"You mean, today?" I asked.

"Well, no, probably not today. What I mean is, everybody passes over to the Third Stage eventually. That'll be something to look forward to, won't it? Seeing your wife and kids again, not to mention your parents and grandparents. What a party that'll be, eh?"

"Oh, uh, they died a while back – my parents and all."

"Right, right," nodded Karac with a smile, "except here we just say, 'passing over.' It's a little like moving from one neighborhood to another."

"What do you mean?"

"Well, your parents for example – they passed over, you know?" Karac looked at me intently. "They don't live on Earth anymore. That's a Stage Two facility. And so now they're in Stage Three. Just like you!"

"You're saying my parents are still alive?"

"Yeah, just like you!" he repeated.

"So, where are they?" I asked doubtfully.

"Not too far away. We'll catch up with them shortly."

"Wait a second. You're saying my parents are here?"

Karac nodded.

"… And I'm here?"

"Right. You made it!"

"So, I'm–"

"Yeah, you passed over," said Karac. "Wasn't so hard, was it? So many Stage Two folks worry their whole lives away over that one small moment – the one day that's always somewhere off in the future. But when you get right down to it, it's a glorious thing, isn't it? Nothing to worry about at all."

Things were starting to make more sense now, even though I hadn't taken the idea of an afterlife seriously since I was in my late teens. "Wow, … I wasn't expecting this," I said, still trying to absorb it all.

"No, not when you rolled out of bed this morning, I'll bet!" Karac said almost jovially.

"And you're sure Cheryl and the kids are okay?"

"Absolutely. You'll soon find that everyone is taken care of properly. Your family will be just fine."

I paused for a few moments before saying, "It's a lot to take in."

"Yeah, yeah. No rush. That's one of the reasons why we're here in Reception. It allows us to compose ourselves a bit – you know, before moving on and meeting the others."

"My folks, you mean?"

"Yeah, we'll get to see them soon enough. Plenty of time. Right now, you and I can visit for a bit and maybe go over any concerns you might have."

"Concerns? Like what?"

"Well, regrets mostly. I mean, Stage Two, that's just a big wide field for learning, and a lot of it comes by making mistakes – you know, doing or saying things we regret later – things we look back on and wish we might have handled differently."

"Oh, I can think of a few of those," I blurted out. For some reason, I felt completely comfortable in the presence of this pleasant stranger. I felt I could tell him anything, fully confident that only good would come of it.

"Right, and so here in Stage Three, it's a good idea to resolve all those things as soon as possible, because this place is eternal, and you don't want to hang onto your regrets forever, right?"

"No, I suppose not. But, what about those things you can't really work through?"

"What do you mean?"

"Well, what about people you don't even know?" I asked as a certain memory suddenly surfaced. "I mean, let's say you offended someone and you never even knew their name. How are you ever going to find them and try to make things right?"

"Oh, don't worry about that," said Karac. "Here, everything gets made right eventually. For example, who did you have in mind?"

"That's what I'm saying. I don't even know her name."

"Knowing a name is the easy part," said Karac. "And her name is Giselle, by the way."

"What??"

"Well, that was your concern just now, wasn't it? Knowing a name? And I'm telling you that knowing a name is no great matter around here. Her name happens to be Giselle."

"But how do you even know who I'm thinking about?" I asked.

"For those willing to pay the price," said Karac, "Stage Three can be like a sea of glass. So many things here are clear and bright and transparent. Anyway, you start telling me the story, and I promise you that in short little while, both you and I will agree her name is Giselle. Fair enough?"

"Fair enough," I said. Sensing an opportunity to unburden myself of one haunting regret, I began telling Karac about the first time I skipped church. Some friends had talked me into seeing a Led Zeppelin concert with them instead.

"I was just seventeen," I said. "Before that, I had only ever been to see Three Dog Night at a family-friendly venue in our town."

"Are you glad you went?" asked Karac. "To the Zeppelin concert, I mean."

"Well, besides *Stairway to Heaven*, I didn't know much about the band, so I didn't really appreciate their music until years later. But, I think it was one of the last shows they ever did in the States, so it's cool that I got to see them."

"That *was* their last U.S. show," said Karac.

"Oh, I think they still had some concerts after that. Chicago and Kansas City, maybe. But yes, I remember that their tour did get cut short. The singer's young son died back in England all of a sudden – something like that."

"Yeah, Robert Plant's son – just five years old. I'm pretty familiar with that story," said Karac, who appeared to bear a much greater resemblance to singer Robert Plant than I had noticed before. "That was just two days after the Oakland show you went to."

"So, they didn't do any more shows in the States?" I asked.

"No, and they only ever did a small handful of concerts after that. England and Germany mostly. And then their drummer, John Bonham, passed over. It's funny, I was just talking to him about all this the other day."

"You know John Bonham?"

"Oh yeah. John and I go way back. He still does some drumming now and then, but mostly he and the others are just waiting for John Paul Jones to arrive before they all get together and start practicing again. But anyway, why don't you tell me more about what happened to you that day – the day of that last Sunday concert."

"After some years went by, I couldn't really remember much about the concert or its music. But what I've never forgotten is how I let people down."

"Like who, for example?" asked Karac.

"Well, besides Giselle, I'd say my mom mostly. She was a woman of such incredible faith and devotion. She didn't say much when I told her about my plans for that Sunday. But her eyes watered up a little, and I knew she was heartbroken. I left the house early that Sunday morning, so I wouldn't have to see her before going to the show. I never went to church again after that. Of course, my mom and I patched things up a long time ago. She understood that kids have to grow up and make their own choices. It was just hard for her to watch, that's all. And I'm sorry that I had to put her through so many heartaches like that for so many years."

"Won't that be something, to get to see her again in a little while?" asked Karac. "She's really excited about it – and your dad too, of course."

There was a light, delicate knock on the door behind Karac.

"And there's somebody else here who's interested in seeing you too," he added.

"Who's that?" I asked.

"It's Giselle," he responded.

"What? The gal from the concert?"

"Yeah, but Giselle doesn't know you saw her there that day or anything. That's a story you can share with her whenever you're ready," said Karac as he got up to answer the door.

"Well, then, why would she be interested in seeing me?" I asked.

"She's looking for a new protégé. Someone who has really studied and appreciates Earth's music. Someone who has attended a lot of amazing and historically important concerts. You see, we do a lot of great music promoting projects here in Stage Three, and I think you and Giselle would make a great team."

At that point, Karac opened the door and quietly stepped out without saying another word. Another short moment passed before a beautiful young woman entered the small room. She was well over a thousand Earth-years old but looked to be in her mid-twenties – just as she had for many centuries.

"Lawrence?" she asked.

"Yes?" I responded, promptly standing up. She was smiling so brightly I strained to see any resemblance to the distressed young lady I had once seen at that Led Zeppelin concert.

"I've heard a lot about you. My name is Giselle," she said. Her face was full of warmth and welcome.

"It's nice to meet you," I said, at a loss for more appropriate words to address this radiant being before me.

"And you as well," she replied with a slight bowing of her head. "How are you feeling?"

"Pretty good, thanks. Although I wasn't really expecting to be in this Third Stage place right now. I mean, it's Wednesday – I think – and I have a couple big projects at the office that I need to take care of. How are they going to get done if I'm supposed to be here now?"

"I can assure you, Lawrence, it won't be long before all those cares disappear like dust in the wind. Besides, you were just a week or two away from retirement, right? Plus, we've got far more enjoyable projects going on around here if you're interested."

"What kind of projects?"

Giselle sat down, and I did too. "I understand you know a thing or two about music," she said.

"A little bit," I replied. "I had a big album collection and some nice audio equipment. I saw lots of shows, especially when I was younger."

"You *are* younger," she said.

"What do you mean?" I asked.

"You're in your prime again. Take a look at your hands."

At Giselle's suggestion, my eyes were drawn to the backs of my hands. They were not nearly as wrinkly and spotted as the last time I took a good look at them.

"What has happened?"

"You've regained your youth. Permanently."

"This is amazing!" I said, trying to grasp all the newness and changes that seemed to be happening all at once.

"You think that's amazing? Just wait until you see your parents. They look a lot like they did on their wedding day!" said Giselle with a little laugh. "Anyway, you were saying you went to a lot of concerts back on Earth."

"Maybe not hundreds of shows like some people, but I went to quite a few."

"I'm envious," said Giselle. "I would love to have seen some shows on Earth. There weren't any big concerts with lots of crowds where I came from."

"And where was that?" I asked.

"Our world was called Deinousse," she said. "There aren't too many Stage Two folks living there anymore."

"You're kidding. You're from a different planet? What's it like there?"

"Well, it's an enormous, old planet and it snows a lot there. But most folks live in this thin equatorial region where it's much warmer and drier. There are lots of flat plains, but there are also many large valleys that could have served as huge natural amphitheaters, except it never occurred to anyone there to use them that way. We're hoping to host some music festivals there in the future," said Giselle.

"Really? Like, who would you have playing there?" I asked.

"Well, I think it would be really great to do some reunion shows with bands from Earth – and bands from lots of other worlds too, of course."

"There are lots of other worlds?"

"So many that you and I couldn't count them. There's so much music out there, you can't even start to comprehend it all just yet. And that's mostly what I'm involved with here in Stage Three. We do collecting, archiving, interpretation, and promotion of music – from all kinds of times and places," she said.

"So, specifically, what bands from Earth would you have playing at these festivals?"

"One of the areas I'm most interested in is late-twentieth-century rock music from Earth. Stuff that's a little more on the progressive side – you know, bands like Kansas, Yes, and the Dixie Dregs."

"You've heard of the Dixie Dregs?" I asked incredulously.

"Oh, yes. They're quite well known here."

"You're kidding! I only met five or six people on Earth who had ever even heard of them."

"Well, ever since Steve Morse arrived a short while ago, he's been playing their tunes and getting the band's name out there. Rock instrumentals have become more popular than ever."

"I can't believe it. This is incredible!" I said.

"Yes, I think you'll like it here. And if you're interested, we could use your help with sound technology preservation."

"What does that mean? What would I be doing?"

"You'd be collecting vintage technology to begin with. Finding, restoring and replicating rare old amplifier vacuum tubes and long-lost specialty stereo needles – things like that."

"That sounds like something I'd be interested in!"

"And then maybe later," said Giselle, "you could move on to becoming a sound technician for concerts and new studio recordings. You'd be working closely with me on projects like that."

"I would love being a concert sound tech! Is that what you do?"

"I used to do some of that. In addition to getting new trainees like you started, my current work is more along the lines of show promotion. I do a lot of public relations work, mediation, contracts, and deals, trying to put reunion shows together – you know, mostly with bands that have been broken up a long time for various reasons."

"How do you do all that?"

"Well, first we track down all the band members. Sometimes they're scattered all over the place. Then we get them talking and working with each other again, and eventually, we have them do a few shows together. We got all six members of Lynyrd Skynyrd from the *Second Helping* album lineup to do a concert not too long ago. It was super. They were really excited about it."

"So, you said you never got to see any of those late twentieth-century bands while they were still on Earth?"

"Not really. I mean, I tried once, but it wasn't a positive experience for someone like me."

"What do you mean?" I asked.

"Deinousse, where I came from, was a very mild, peaceful place. Survival there in the equatorial regions was not very difficult at all. The people were very passive and simple and friendly – not unlike life here in Stage Three, really. Anyway, long after I left Deinousse, I tried going to a concert on Earth once and, well, ... I guess I just wasn't prepared for the kind of environment I found there. It was a very different type of place than the one I was used to," said Giselle.

"Was that a Led Zeppelin concert in California?" I asked.

"Yes, how did you know?"

"Because I was there too," I said. "I saw you. You went right past me in a state of awful panic and distress, and I did nothing."

"You were there – at that concert?"

"Yeah, and I have had regrets about that day for all these years, and I just want to tell you that I'm sorry. I'm so sorry that I just stood there, holding my place so I could see some stupid show when I should have helped you get out of that crowd."

"But you didn't know who I was," said Giselle.

"How would that matter one way or the other? I could see you were in a bad state and there were all these people laughing at you and making fun of you when you went past."

"But you weren't one of them, were you?"

"No," I said.

"And you weren't doing any of the pinching and grabbing as I went by, right?"

"No."

"So, you had a little decency and compassion then, wouldn't you say?"

82

"Not nearly as much as I should have," I said, still quite angry with myself.

"But, after that experience, would you have acted differently if you found yourself in the same situation again?" asked Giselle.

"Of course! I would have grabbed your hand and pushed through that tightly packed crowd 'til I got you to a safer area."

"And that's what this Third Stage place – Eternity – is all about. It's about reconciliation. It's about forgiveness. It's about moving forward with no more regrets, because we learn from our errors, improve our behaviors, and become better people in the process."

"Yeah, well I think I will probably still be kicking myself over that experience for a long time."

"There's no need," said Giselle. "Look at me. All the tears have been dried. I am here. I am safe. I am happy. And you should be happy too. It's a great and glorious day for you if you think about it for a moment. Now, how about if we go see your parents?"

"Oh, that would be wonderful!" I said, "I thought I would never see them again!"

"And if you learn to relax and quit kicking yourself, I'll make sure you see the first Led Zeppelin reunion show when John Paul Jones gets here in a few more Earth-years. How's that?"

Chapter 9: Timeless

I have never in my life made music for money or fame ...
No way. God walks out of the room when you're thinking about money.
Quincy Jones

Earth-year 2033

"Here, try this," I said, helping Giselle fit a newly-refurbished set of bulky, 1970s, padded headphones over her ears. I set the stereo needle just before the last track, and she listened through the slight hiss and small crackles before the music got underway. When it did, she gave a little jump, as if half-startled. Before long, a grin appeared on her face, and it got bigger and bigger as the tune progressed. About three-quarters through *Frankenstein*, Giselle began hearing all kinds of delightfully pointed synthesizer pops and squeals that seemed to attack her head from all angles even though she was only hearing them stereophonically through her two ears. She was all smiles.

"That's The Edgar Winter Group, isn't it? I've heard that tune before, but never like this, Lawrence!"

"Amazing, isn't it?" I responded. "That's how it's meant to be heard, with a good set of headphones. Put those on again and close your eyes, I have some more stuff for you to listen to."

I pulled out a copy of The Tubes' first album and gently laid the shiny black vinyl onto the turntable. The first two tracks, *Up from the Deep* and *Haloes* join together perfectly as if they are one long tune. They are always best played together – seamlessly, back-to-back – a feat never quite accomplished with "advanced" CD technology.

"That's kind of a quirky start," she said, opening her eyes.

"Shhhhh," I said. "Just give it a moment."

Before long, Giselle was enjoying similar strafings of synthesizer sounds swirling around and around her head. String and horn arrangements joined in. And then *Haloes* started up with a light jazz groove before Prairie Prince began his beautifully relentless attack on the drums, creating a giant crescendo of tension and energy. For Giselle, the music ended all too quickly. I lifted the needle from the groove before the album's third track got underway.

"Wow!" said Giselle as she took the heavy headphones off, "What *was* that?"

"Well, first let me ask you – Can you tell what time period it came from?"

"I have no idea," she responded after a long pause.

"And that's what I like most about these tunes. They're timeless," I said.

"They're powerful!" said Giselle.

"Unfortunately," I went on, "some tunes let you know exactly when they were made because they're stuck there."

"But isn't that because they're tied to certain memories and events from earlier days?" she asked.

"Yeah, and that's fine. I mean, I like music for lots of different reasons, and nostalgia is certainly one of them. But what I'm saying is, some pieces of music seem stuck in time because they were specifically made for that time. They were made to fit in. They were made to be popular. To make money. And they started sounding old just a few months or years after they were recorded."

"So, what keeps these timeless pieces from sounding dated?" asked Giselle.

"Maybe because some composers were so confident their music would be better appreciated with the passing of time, they were willing to forego immediate fame and popularity. I remember jazz pianist Thelonious Monk once saying you should write and play the music that's true to you even if it takes the public a couple decades to understand it."

"You'd have to feel your music was truly inspired to have that kind of nerve and confidence."

"Yeah, I think it took real guts and some risk to write the inspired stuff because your work might become lost and forgotten in a dusty old attic trunk someplace. That's where I found that Tubes album a short while ago – in Elk Falls, Kansas, of all places. I had never heard that LP before."

"I'm glad you found it," said Giselle. "That's some fantastic stuff!"

"Well, this is the best job I've ever had," I said, "digging up some of these inspired pieces and bringing them back to life. They always sound surprisingly fresh. They have stood the test of time."

"And time certainly is a test, isn't it? I'm glad we don't have to deal with it any longer," said Giselle.

"Yeah, ironically, that combination of time and mortality was both music's greatest friend and its worst of enemies. It was pain and suffering, along with the contrasting joys of mortality, that brought out some of the most beautiful, heartfelt music. On the other hand, just think of how illness, death, accidents, greed, egos, pride, and arguments have crushed music's greatest potential on so many occasions."

"It's a wonder that so much of it ever saw the light of day," observed Giselle. "It's a wonder that we're able to collect and preserve so much of it now."

"And there's so much Earth music left to collect," I went on. "The late 1950s ushered in a few decades of imaginative, inspired, free-spirited music unlike any previous age on Earth. Talent was so abundant and came so easily to so many composers that some didn't fully understand or appreciate their own music at the time. Some bands faded fast because they didn't take their own inspired music as seriously as they should have. Under the pressures of mortality, many bands quickly flashed and then disappeared. Rock music was readily dismissed by too many as a noisy, passing fad. But, here in this Stage Three environment, some of these lost and forgotten bands are getting new chances to reach their full potential."

"But some bands lasted quite a long time in mortality, didn't they?" asked Giselle. "I mean, look at the Rolling Stones – touring and putting out new LPs for over fifty Earth-years."

"Yeah, they certainly figured out how to survive the ravages of time and mortality," I said in agreement. "I remember when my buddy Dave went to see The Rolling Stones in concert – on Mick Jagger's thirty-fifth birthday no less! 'Are you kidding?' I said to myself. 'Those old guys??' Absolutely no one in the late 1970s predicted Mick Jagger and Paul McCartney would still be selling out stadium shows three decades later. It was unthinkable! I can tell you for sure that the Rolling Stones never foresaw that future!"

"How did that happen, do you think?" asked Giselle. "How were they able to keep their success and popularity going for such a long time?"

"Well," I mused, "that explosively creative era of composition was followed by a relative musical void that had folks desperately clinging to that former age like a lifeboat. And the more time passed, the more people had to acknowledge that bands like the Rolling Stones wouldn't live forever there on Earth. So, many fans would take the opportunity of seeing and hearing them 'one last time.' There were so many 'one last times' with that band. It was incredible! And people wanted a piece of that. They wanted a piece of the unthinkable, the impossible. They wanted immortality."

"And now we have it," said Giselle, "but there is still so much demand to see bands perform live."

"It's interesting, isn't it?" I responded. "I think in addition to being entertained by great music, it's thrilling for people to see – and almost touch – iconic figures like that. It brings them a sense of connection and unity with millions of others who also love their music."

"I guess those fans all become like this huge collective family in a way – tied together by this musical experience and mutual appreciation," added Giselle.

"Yeah, people like that bond. They want to see the real deal. And with the Rolling Stones, you had this huge core of band members who had mostly been together since the beginning – since 1962. They're the ones with the stories. They're the ones who originally wrote the music under the various pressures and constraints of mortality. They're the ones who went through all the discussions and arguments and fistfights together in the studios trying to put those albums together. It was their blood, sweat, and tears that made us all happy. A tribute band can't claim any of that experience or soul no matter how well they imitate the sound. There are innovators, and there are imitators."

"Play another one of those timeless pieces for me," said Giselle as she put the bulky headphones back on. She was tired of hearing me ramble away, I suppose.

An exotically complex piece came to mind, and I went over to one of the many shelves of vinyl LP's in that room and pulled out a copy of *Relayer*, by Yes. The cover artwork by Roger Dean brought back memories of trying to copy his fantasy illustration style in my young mortal days.

"Okay. Here's one you might like. 'Timeless' means it will sound good forever," I said as I dropped the needle onto Side Two. "This one's called *Sound Chaser*."

But by then Giselle had closed her eyes in preparation for a good listen, and all she heard from me were muffled sounds.

Chapter 10: Sound Chaser

*I play the notes as they are
written, but it is God who makes the music.*
Johann Sebastian Bach

Baja California Peninsula – November 1710

Ta'a Neh was looked upon as the most talented of musicians, and therefore, he was his people's primary choice to entertain the newly-arrived visitors from an exotic, faraway land. He would represent the finest of culture that his people had to offer, and unfortunately, there was little else to offer except for their cherished black biscuits. The thought of helping to provide both gifts was pleasing to Ta'a Neh as he squatted over a large, flat desert rock – just as his people had done for centuries.

The season of the pitahaya fruit was nearing its very end when the great white sails of a British ship first appeared from the south. The annual ripening of the sweet oozing fruit with its many seeds, hidden in a ball of protruding cactus spikes, was always cause for weeks of autumn celebration. There were now only a few small samples of the wild fruit remaining – to be collected and reserved for the chief elders, and for revered, spiritually-gifted musicians like Ta'a Neh.

He was unaware that, a short time before, a few of the wonderfully-dressed visitors had chanced upon the sight of an elder squatting naked over that very same flat stone. Facing away from the three young men, the aged one could tell there were strangers not far behind him but could not detect that they were pointing at him with crude humor borne of obvious superiority. Theirs was the mocking of a lesser being, whose defecation onto the flat rock seemed comically primitive.

Several other flat stones nearby, used for the same purpose, had already begun to offer up the season's second harvest. The scorching sun by day and the occasional sprinkle of rain at night had dried up and washed away most all other matter, leaving behind black, shiny, undigested pitahaya seeds. Millions of them.

The ship's lookout spotted campfires far down the shore the previous evening and correctly presumed they glowed near a source of fresh water. The vessel's captain, Rodger Woods, along with his fellow privateers, had no means of effectively communicating with the natives of the Baja California Peninsula, but were determined to head ashore the following afternoon in search of refreshment. The astonished tribal elders warmly greeted the magnificent visitors as their rowboats came aground but had little food to offer beyond some small bony fish and bicuits. The last of the season's pitahaya fruit was carefully kept out of sight.

Still, there was a desire to gain the favor of these strangers who apparently possessed great wealth and power. With hand gestures, the elders invited Captain Woods and his crew to sit and hear the finest of musical performances. In the light of the evening campfire, Ta'a Neh came forward with his instruments. He slowly seated himself cross-legged on the dusty ground and closed his eyes.

A hymn softly began to lift from his throat. It was a mildly melodic prayer to Niparaja, thanking the god for the honor of these strangers' visit, and asking for them to be blessed with health, and food, and for calm sea weather in their travels. As he sang, Ta'a Neh took his two musical wands in hand. They had been notched until they produced the perfect accompanying tone when dragged across one another. Tears began to tickle the corners of his eyes as the hymn filled Ta'a Neh with gratitude for the visit of these beautiful deities. He was certain this spiritual euphoria would flow from him and be felt by all present around the campfire.

"They are the most pathetic of wretches," Captain Woods would later write in his log book. "We were entertained, as it was supposed, by a dull figure who hummed a flat tune and poorly kept time with two old sticks."

Near the completion of his hymn, Ta'a Neh slowly opened his eyes and was perplexed to find that his audience was not moved in the intended, expected manner. Instead, there were slight grins and knowing nudges of superiority. Surely these beings, with their magnificent sea vessels, clothing, footwear, and other finely crafted objects, were accustomed to music vastly superior to his own.

Ta'a Neh felt the imperative to try harder to please his audience, to humbly invoke the swelling, encompassing spirit with two more sacred hymns of praise, blessing, and gratitude. But afterward the visitors' countenances had not changed in the slightest, and Ta'a Neh's sense of shame was only partially alleviated by the offering of his people's prized biscuits to these guests.

Captain Woods continued to write, "We were finally given some crusts, surprisingly delicate in flavor but lacking consistent form or much substance. We freely consumed, being desirous for bread, and these morsels having the appearance of dark rye."

Another prized seasonal delicacy for Ta'a Neh's people, and a precious gift to be offered to such wondrous guests, the thin biscuits had just been baked onto the surface of smooth, round, fire-heated stones. Mixed into a paste with a little water, the biscuits' dark, coarse flour had been ground from millions of pitahaya seeds collected from the flat desert rocks – autumn's second harvest.

Later that night, after the visitors returned to their anchored vessel, Ta'a Neh sat on the beach viewing the masts in the moonlight and seeing the occasional golden lantern glow on the deck. Even before the arrival of the British ship, he knew there must be greater, more majestic forms of music, but his culture had no words to describe the sounds Ta'a Neh longed to hear and play, and no means to create them. Now, for the first time, his ears caught thrilling snatches of fiddle and squeezebox as they floated back to him over the coastal waters.

By morning the ship was gone. The short remainder of Ta'a Neh's mortal life, when not devoted to food gathering, was tirelessly spent chasing those musical sounds, trying to duplicate them with constant experimentation. His closest successes were short chordal whistlings from cut, dried reeds swung through the air with a thin leather strap. Although his society kept no track of numbered years, an old, deeply wrinkled Ta'a Neh would die elderly and revered before the age of thirty-six. They mourned his passing, bestowing upon him a new name that meant Sound Chaser, and honoring him as the greatest musician they had ever known. His body was left to the elements with arms folded carefully across his chest, securing his set of dried musical reeds.

******

Under the tutelage of Smalls, Giselle, and other angelic beings, Ta'a Neh learned much about music and cultures during the Earth-centuries that followed his mortal life – all to his great delight. Not only did he compose great works himself, but he became anxiously engaged in the eternal work of his mentors. Ta'a Neh grew remarkably fluent in numerous languages, and well-versed in a variety of manners, customs, and clothing from several worlds. His favorite assignments were those related to his home planet, Earth, and he would often revisit the place – either incognito or assuming various personas – performing acts of divine intervention.

Not all of them went well, however. Ta'a Neh would shake his head with disappointment every time he thought of his failures. The first one was the most serious and painful of them all. Ta'a Neh was perfectly positioned to prevent the sudden fall that brought deafness to Ludwig van Beethoven in 1798. Unfortunately, he was momentarily distracted from this assignment by the tunes of a street musician coming in from one of Beethoven's windows.

Then there was the time Ta'a Neh misunderstood a street address and got lost in a busy part of town. He arrived at his destination a few minutes too late, missing an opportunity to get heated buses for Buddy Holly's Winter Dance Party Tour in early 1959. As a result, Buddy Holly and others took an ill-fated plane ride to the next show, cutting a potentially vast musical legacy short with a fatal crash in a snowy, Iowa cornfield.

But Ta'a Neh also felt he had some great successes to celebrate. One of them was encouraging Freddie Mercury and Queen to perform at the Live Aid benefit concert at Wembley Stadium in 1985.

Another memorable assignment was locating and purchasing parts of the old spaceship stage used by Electric Light Orchestra on their *Out of the Blue* tour in 1978. Ta'a Neh obtained the parts from a scrapyard whose owners no longer knew what they were or where they came from. They would later be used as a design prototype for building a new saucer-shaped stage – one that would actually fly. It was hoped that a *real* flying saucer stage would motivate ELO to perform together again someday.

Ta'a Neh's favorite assignment though was encouraging Patrick Moraz to leave his band, Refugee, in 1974. The idea was to have him replace Rick Wakeman who had just left Yes as the group started recording their *Relayer* album that same year. By that time, Ta'a Neh knew full well that there were descendants of Captain Roger Woods' crew among the band of British progressive rock musicians. It tickled him to recall that, Earth-centuries earlier, he had once fed their disrespectful sailor ancestors bread that had already passed through his own digestive tract. If only they had known!

Best of all, Ta'a Neh broke a rule that prohibited angelic beings from leaving personal traces of their missions' successes. Ta'a Neh could not help the further impish pleasure and satisfaction of convincing Yes to christen their most complex *Relayer* track with a title that had special meaning to him. They called it *Sound Chaser*.

Chapter 11: Reminiscing

Now as the years roll on, each time we
hear our favorite song, the memories come along.
Graeham Goble

Earth-year 2091

"I've been working on this gig for eons," said Giselle. That claim was nothing but an exaggeration as eons aren't really an accurate measurement in eternity. But if you want to talk Earth-years, it had only been a few decades. "And you know what, Lawrence?" she continued, "I've got it pretty much locked up, finally!"

"The LRB deal, you mean?"

"Yes, can you believe it? And it's the 1979 lineup! No one has even come remotely close to putting all those guys together before."

"Who's playing bass?" I asked.

"Take your pick," said Giselle. "I've got George McArdle and Barry Sullivan both standing by."

Either one would do, I thought, reaching back for a moment into some of the deepest corners of my memory. I recalled the strange, empty feeling on that cold night near the end of 1979. Something just wasn't right.

"Maybe we got here way early," I said to Janna hopefully as we pulled into the Convention Center's parking area. I had been to enough concerts by then to know I had just made a ridiculously impossible statement. Even at an event that had assigned seating, there was no such thing as too early. Not at this hour. More lights should have been on. The marquee should have been lit up. There should have been people hanging around outside. There should have been more than just a lonely car or two out in the large parking lot.

Instead, the street lights shined down through seasonally bare trees onto empty, silent asphalt.

"Maybe they moved the show to another place," said Janna, just as hopefully.

"Yeah, maybe," I replied. I wasn't sure of anything at that odd moment.

After circling the building a couple more times in disbelief, I finally parked and got out of the car. I pulled on the cold metal handles of the sizeable double-door entryway, but they didn't budge. I checked another door and one after that with the same result. It was with incredulous frustration that I pounded on the last door hoping to get some sort of answer. After all, I was there on my first date with Janna, and I knew she liked the Little River Band even more than I did. Having purchased prime seats weeks in advance, and at some expense, this had been my chance to make a big impression on her. I pounded on the door one more time and waited.

To my surprise, the door opened slightly, and a short, older-looking maintenance man poked his bald head out. The hall behind him was dark and completely quiet. "Is this where the Little River Band is playing tonight?" I asked, doubtful at that point.

The look on the man's face gave the answer before his reply. "No, sir. There are no shows here tonight."

I showed the man my tickets. "Look, it says the Convention Center, and that's today's date, right?" The man couldn't help but agree I was at the right place at the right time.

"But, I'm sorry, sir," he repeated. "There are no shows here tonight." There was nothing more he could do.

Talking more to myself than to the maintenance man, I said, "Something's not right. There should be others here who are also thinking they've got the right time and place."

Wanting to end the hopeless conversation with a potential resolution, the older man said, "Well, you might try calling the ticket agency, and see what they say."

"Yes, I'll do that. Thanks," I said quietly as I started to walk away.

"Well," I said to Janna as I got back in the car, "this is the right day and the right time for the show, but for some reason, it's not happening here like it's written on the tickets." I spread them in front of her, hoping she'd clearly see I had not made some horribly grievous mistake. Just the same, I was mortified. "I'll just call the ticket agency and find out what's going on. If it's someplace else, we still have time to get there." Janna gave a genuinely encouraging smile. A few blocks away was a phone booth, and I was pleased to find folks at the ticket agency office still answering phones at that hour.

"I'm sorry," said the woman on the other end of the line, "but there is no Little River Band show tonight."

"But I've got my tickets right here," I said, "They say tonight, Friday night, at the Convention Center."

"Let's see. Let me just check something," said the woman. "Oh yes, it says here that the show *was* originally scheduled for tonight, but it got rescheduled to last night at the Convention Center."

"Last night? So, it's over?? We missed it?? Why didn't I know about this earlier? I would have changed my plans!" I suppose the growing anger in my voice sounded as if it were the woman's fault that the concert date had changed.

"I'm sorry, sir," she responded calmly. "It says here there were radio announcements about the change."

"It changed to the night before? From a Friday night to a Thursday night?" I asked in exasperated disbelief.

"I'm sorry, sir," said the woman. "We're closing now, but you'll be able to get a full cash refund at any ticket sales desk tomorrow when they open."

I hung up the phone and humbly returned to the car to explain the situation to Janna. We tried to laugh it off, but the two of us never went out on a date again, and I never saw the Little River Band in concert. But Janna did. She ended up marrying a nerdy little guy with red hair and gobs of freckles who, incidentally, was successful in taking her to see the Little River Band. That was less than a year after my failed attempt and I never really had a good opportunity to see that band ever again.

My thoughts returned to Giselle and her enthusiastic news about finally getting the Little River Band back together again. It gave me hope that I might be able to see them in concert after all.

"That's incredible!" I said, "So you're getting LRB back together. When was the last time Shorrock and Goble even spoke to one another?"

"It has been a long, long while," she replied, "but they've both tentatively agreed to seven rehearsal sessions and two live shows."

"How did you get them on board?"

"You'll never guess how easy it was. Vegemite!"

"What?"

"You know, 'She just smiled and gave me a Vegemite sandwich,'" Giselle responded with a familiar melody.

"Yeah, but what is that stuff?"

"You don't know? I mean, you've never tried it?"

"Uh, … no," I replied. "I was an American. We didn't have Vegemite in the States."

"But, that 'land down under' song – it held the number one position in the U.S. for about a month."

"Maybe that was part of the song's appeal," I suggested, "talking about exotic, Australian foods like Vegemite. I don't know."

"Well, anyway, Goble's crazy about the stuff and I found out he's been craving it ever since he passed over."

"So, where on earth did you get the Vegemite?" I asked.

"It wasn't on *Earth*," Giselle grinned. "I've got friends in particularly high places, you know."

I certainly did know. Somehow Giselle was able to present me with a big bag of nacho cheese flavored tortilla chips once. It felt like I hadn't had some of those for several millennia.

"Anyway," Giselle continued, "after four rehearsals Goble gets one Vegemite sandwich, another one when all seven rehearsals have been completed, and then a case of twenty jars after the two shows are over. And, of course, there are potential bonus jars based on crowd appreciation and all that."

"So, the band gets rewarded for crowd-pleasing?" I asked.

"Absolutely," said Giselle. "The rewards are based on applause decibel levels. The band can't just go through the motions. Not like they would or anything, but there's nothing wrong with providing a little extra incentive to put on a good show, right?"

Giselle knew what she was talking about. The best word to describe her eternal vocation was *impresario*. She worked as an agent, negotiator, and producer, all in one, putting concerts and music shows together. And although Giselle's home planet, Deinousse, was several universes away, her area of musical specialty was planet Earth, from the 1950s to the 1990s. That's how I ended up as her protégé. Not only was Earth my home planet but I had personally witnessed many great concerts during the second half of that era. Unfortunately, there were a few shows that I missed too, and like septillions and octillions of other people now, wished that I could have attended. I happened to mention to Giselle once in passing about missing the Little River Band concert at the Convention Center that one night. Being a fan herself, she made a mental note of the void and sought to fill it with a reunion show.

"And what about Birtles and Shorrock?" I asked. "What do they want?"

"Birtles is happy enough just doing the gig. He hasn't really demanded anything. But Shorrock, … he won't sing unless the venue is an exact replica of the Sydney Opera House. And that's way easier than coming up with the

Vegemite I might add. The problem is size. So many people want to see these shows, and the Opera House only holds, what … twenty-five … twenty-six hundred? We're still in talks with him to see if we can replicate the Opera House on a larger scale and fit ten times as many people inside."

"Do you think he'll go for it?" I asked.

"I hope so," said Giselle, "he's holding the key to any reunion concerts, or at least that's what he's been saying ever since his Earth days."

"What does he mean by that?"

"I think he means, even though everyone else in the band might be interested in reuniting, it won't happen without him."

"You might have to go with an original-sized replica of the Sydney Opera House."

"That's a fair possibility," sighed Giselle

"And that would further reduce my chances of ever seeing them," I said.

"Yes, it would," said Giselle, "except that you're going to be the assistant sound technician for that show!"

"I am? How did that happen?"

"It's my show. I'm putting it together, and I can bring in any production helpers I want," she said with a smile.

"Are you kidding?"

"Nope. Your days of rummaging through landfills and junkyards looking for vintage stereo parts are over. It's time for you to move on to bigger and better things – like being a concert and studio sound tech!"

******

Not long after, Glenn Shorrock agreed to perform with the reunited, 1979 lineup of the Little River Band. He even agreed to a larger scale replica of the Sydney Opera House that seated nearly twelve thousand.

The chief sound technician, Quincy Jones, and I ran through the sound check that evening and got the balance perfect before I went backstage for a quick visit with Giselle.

"This is so great!" I exclaimed. "Thank you so much for putting all this together, Giselle. I think this may just turn out better than that show I missed back in '79!"

"Oh, you're welcome," she said, "I just wish I could have gotten regular house seats for you and Cheryl. With the seating lottery system for these types of limited events, our best bet for seeing these shows comes with our work in putting them together."

I nodded. From the sound booth, Cheryl and I would actually have some of the very best seats in the house. Before I left the backstage area, I parted the burgundy-colored curtains slightly to view the immensity of the newly-constructed Opera House replica. And then I saw someone who looked familiar taking her seat in the center of the fourth or fifth row. I squinted my eyes a bit for a better look. It couldn't be ... But it was! It was Janna! She was there at the Little River Band reunion show! And sitting next to her was her nerdy-looking, red-headed husband who still had gobs of freckles.

Chapter 12: Up from the Deep

But he knows not that the dead are there;
and that her guests are in the depths of hell.
Proverb of Solomon

Wingen, New South Wales, Australia – 1829

"It's not volcanic?"

"No," said Reverend Wilton, surveying the smoky landscape. "All the evidence points to coal, burning underground. Who knows how deep or for how long?" Other geologists would eventually determine that the coal seam at Wingen Hill burned nearly ten stories below the earth's surface and had been doing so for millennia.

"Coal burns underground? Without air?" asked Mr. Thomlinson.

"It's just smoldering, really," came Wilton's reply, "But you see, just as the smoke makes its way to the surface, those same types of gaps and channels are drawing air deep into the ground. I'm sure there are all kinds of pockets and tunnels and caverns in the sandstone beneath us."

Mr. Thomlinson pondered the thought for a moment and then offered an idea he felt had already crossed the Reverend's mind. "Do you suppose – right below us – is the location of Hell itself? Wouldn't that be something, to be standing directly on top of it?"

Reverend Wilton, a man of both faith and science, did indeed have a similar, fleeting thought a short time before, but did not race to give an answer. Instead, he smiled and looked downward, passing the toe of his boot back and forth over one of the many small belches of smoke emerging from the ground beneath him.

"Do you suppose, my dear friend," Wilton said at last, "that there is any sin, any infraction, any misdeed, that would justify the suffering of burning for all of eternity?"

"Well, I–"

"Think of history's most notorious villains," Reverend Wilton continued. "Caligula, Nero, Atilla, Herod. Even after having killed hundreds or thousands of innocents, do you suppose they would be consigned to eternal suffering?"

"Not only for their many murders, yes, but one cannot count all the sufferings they have caused," countered Mr. Thomlinson.

"Ah, but one can, my good man. Not with numerals perhaps, but consider for a moment – have not all those sufferings come to an end by now, after these many hundreds of years and the passing of all who suffered?"

"I suppose so," Thomlinson conceded.

"Then you would agree those sufferings are finite in number. And yet, eternity is infinite. An eternity in Hell for a few years of demonic behavior would hardly be the dispensing of pure, godly justice, I should say."

"But surely if there is to be justice at all, then some form of punishment or restriction should exist."

"Certainly," said Reverend Wilton, "but rest assured dear Thomlinson, we are not standing on top of Hell. This is merely a burning coal seam. No souls are suffering beneath our feet."

Concerning that very last notion, the good Reverend was ignorantly mistaken. For in the dark pockets, tunnels and caverns below were at least eleven souls – all suffering in silence, smoke, darkness, and solitude. Nearly 180 years later, another lonely soul would join them.

******

Atkinson, New Hampshire, USA – 2007

In his current state of existence, (a spirit which had not yet regained a resurrected body), Vince was unable to fully cry.

There were no tears to cry with. But certainly, he felt the full anguish of the moment. Anxiety swelled inside him as he watched Brad move about the house with purpose and determination.

Vince didn't feel very much like a "saving angel," as those with his specific assignment are sometimes called. In fact, there was no apparent saving to be done at this moment. In most respects, Vince was helpless – unable to communicate or otherwise prevent the act of desperation unfolding before him. He could only observe and hope to discover the whereabouts of a fellow soul following a self-inflicted departure. He knew from personal experience that they could be difficult to find sometimes.

Brad closed the bathroom door leaving the invisible, undetectable Vince out in the hallway with the cat. A short time later, he turned off the lights and reclined on the bathroom floor. Brad reached back to tug the pillow more fully up under his neck. He crossed his ankles, folded his arms, closed his eyes and resolutely waited. "Don't look back," he said to himself. "Don't look back."

If there was an element of peace to this moment, it came as the result of careful preparation. Brad mentally reviewed all the steps in sequence, starting with the purchase of several items from the local home improvement store. Among them were two small barbecue grills, a can of lighter fluid, a large bag of charcoal and a roll of duct tape. "If you can't fix it with duct tape, you're not using enough duct tape," he recalled hearing once on some comedy show. But for Brad, there was hardly any humor left in the saying. All the duct tape in the world couldn't fix his troubles, but perhaps a roll of it could help end his profound pain and sorrow. It was more than a feeling. It was as if some kind of soul-eating bacteria was consuming him from the inside out.

The car, the keys, the doors (some purposely locked and others deliberately unlocked), were all arranged for the benefit of those who would show up later looking for Brad. Then there were the four handwritten notes of caution, explanation, and instruction for easy discovery by all concerned friends and loved ones. Three of them were thoughtfully placed in strategic locations to reduce all potential shock to a minimum. He remembered to grab a pillow from the bed and casually tossed it on the bathroom floor as he headed back to the car for the supplies.

He carried the two small barbecue grills upstairs to the bathroom and set them in the tub beside the bag of charcoal. The cat had wandered in, rubbing itself against his legs. Brad sadly and carefully set the cat out in the hallway, not far from the unseen Vince, then went back into the bathroom and closed the door.

Using his teeth, Brad tore the plastic wrapper from the newly-purchased roll of duct tape. Once opened, he pulled long sticky stretches of the silvery-gray material and worked them into the bathroom window seams. As an afterthought, he taped over the entire window pane as well, blocking any light from the outside. With the window sealed, Brad turned and faced the closed bathroom door, taping all four of its outer edges as well. Deciding not to take any chances, he taped up all the electrical outlets and the bathroom fan vent until they were airtight.

Ripping open the corner of the charcoal bag was less challenging than opening the duct tape. Brad tipped the bottom of the bag upwards and evenly poured the briquettes into the barbecue grill basins.

Before applying the lighter fluid and starting the flame; before turning out the lights; before reclining on the floor, Brad fastened the fourth of his handwritten notes to his collar. It read, "J'ai une âme solitaire. I am a lonely soul."

Oxygen was consumed. Carbon monoxide intensified. Brad's throat stung with smoke. His eyes smarted too and began to tear up, starting a short wail of sadness as he prepared to let his life go. Instead of the beautiful high notes he was once famous for, there was coughing.

The floor beneath him melted away, along with the stinging of the smoke and the comfort of the pillow. The sorrow was still there, only he was unable to fully cry. There were no longer any tears to cry with. The only sensation, beyond the ongoing sadness, was an awareness – awareness of darkness and self in a small, unfamiliar place. Brad kept his eyes closed, hoping to evaporate into complete nothingness. But that hope was never fully realized. He had somehow merely traded one form of dark, smoky confinement for another, thousands of miles away. Brad eased into a coma-like state. It was several months before Vince was able to locate him – in a coal seam pocket burning deep beneath a hill in the Southern Hemisphere.

******

Wingen, New South Wales, Australia – 2008

"Brad?"

Brad heard his name being called, but not with his ears. No physical voice had caused air to vibrate, nor sound to ripple, but Brad was aware of his name being spoken just the same. The voice was louder than the slight, muffled moans of pain that occasionally came from similarly lost souls nearby, and louder than those regretful moans that sometimes arose from within himself. He opened his eyes and saw nothing but utter darkness.

"Brad? Are you there?"

Brad kept still. He was as close to oblivion as he could hope for and didn't want that ruined. Perhaps with the passing of a little more time, uninterrupted by visitors, his existence would completely dissolve away. Still, it was intriguing that someone should say his name after so long, especially here in this dark, unfamiliar place.

"Brad. It's me. Vince. We've met a couple times before."

Met before? Brad had probably met a thousand fans named Vince. What would one of them be doing here, of all places? No good could possibly come from it. Brad did not answer, hoping the unwanted guest would become discouraged and wander away.

"Yeah, for a while there I was with the Dead." Vince barely finished the sentence before he started laughing. "Sounds funny to say that now!"

Brad failed to understand the comment and the humor behind it but stayed silent.

"And you were with Boston, right? Anyway," Vince went on, "we met backstage once at Madison Square Garden."

Brad couldn't recall the meeting. Was this person talking about the Grateful Dead? Was this their keyboard player, Vince, speaking to him?

"Before that," said Vince, "we nearly opened for you guys in San Francisco once, but that show got postponed for some reason, and we lost the gig. That was in '78 or '79, I think. I was with The Tubes then."

Brad Delp suddenly recalled a sad article he had read several months before carrying those charcoal grills upstairs to his bathroom. It was about a fellow musician – a keyboard player named Vince Welnick – who had also taken his own life.

"But, you know, all the fame, all the money, all the exotic traveling – it doesn't always add up to happiness, does it?" said Vince.

Brad began to squirm with the reawakening of emotional pain.

"You can be surrounded by adoring fans and loving friends and family, and still be a lonely soul," Vince went on.

Brad felt the full piercing of those words, especially the last three.

"Une âme solitaire," Vince softly, but purposely, repeated in French.

"Who are you?!" Brad finally yelled in exasperation. "What are you doing here?!"

"I'm here to walk home with you," said Vince.

"Home?! I'm not going anywhere!" shouted Brad, and then after a few moments of silence, his voice turned quiet. "Please, can you please just leave me alone? I just want to be alone."

Vince also allowed a few moments of pause before saying, "You can't do it, can you? You can't even be upset with someone without saying 'Please' or 'Thank you' or 'Excuse me' or 'I'm sorry.' You know, after you left, all anybody could say was, 'He was the nicest guy in the business.' Everybody loved you."

"Not everybody," said Brad.

"Hey, well, business is business. Band lineups get changed and all that. And for some of us, it's crushing, 'cause it's like losing family sometimes. Man, I didn't even get invited to the Grateful Dead Family Reunion show, and I was with them about five years. I can tell you, that hurt! That hurt–"

"It wasn't all about Boston," interrupted Brad.

"What do you mean?" asked Vince.

"It wasn't all about the band."

"The talk went around that you and guitarist Tom weren't getting along – that your musical input wasn't accepted like it used to be. And some were saying you were frustrated over not being able to sing those super high notes anymore."

"Well, maybe some of that's true, but maybe people don't know what they're talking about sometimes. They don't know the whole story. There were personal matters."

"And they brought you to the point of ending it all?"

"I'm not sure how any of this is your business. Besides, didn't you do a little number on your own self a while back?"

Vince gave thoughtful pause before replying, "Yes, and maybe because of that, I know what it's like to be a lonely soul. Maybe I'm the one who has the best chance of bringing you back."

"I'm not going back anywhere," said Brad. "I can't face 'em! Don't you understand?"

"Who can't you face?"

"The people I've let down. The people I've hurt. My fiancée. My family. My friends. I can't go back!"

"Did you love them?"

"Of course, I loved them!" said Brad. "I still do! That's the problem! That's what I can't face! I've thought terrible things. I've done terrible things … And now I've let them all down even more by running away." After a few moments he added, "Anyway, I don't expect they love me much anymore."

"Are you kidding? Of course, they–"

"But I've broken their trust, and you can never get that back again."

"Never? I don't think so."

"And how would you know one way or the other?" asked Brad.

"One thing I do know, eternity is huge! Think about it for a minute. Eternity is so big that everyone becomes reconciled and every offence gets forgiven eventually."

"Maybe, but how do you ever gain someone's trust back once it's lost? How can I ever learn to trust *myself* again? I mean, I've had bouts of depression and thoughts of suicide ever since I was a teenager. How can I get past all of that?"

"It starts by letting go of everything – the deepest, darkest parts of ourselves."

Brad kept still for a couple of moments before responding. "It's true that there are parts of me I don't want anymore. I suppose that's what I was trying to run away from. But I think I made things all the worse by taking my own life."

Brad paused for another moment or so. "I feel sick about myself sometimes," he said. "I mean, I've been a decent person for the most part, but I've made some dreadful errors in judgment. In moments of severe loneliness, I've had terrible thoughts and sometimes I've acted in ways that even I can't completely fathom."

"Now you're starting to see and acknowledge your weaknesses," said Vince. "That is the first great step away from the darkness."

"Yeah, well, it might be okay for me and you to be sitting here talking like this, but I don't think I can face everyone else about all these things."

"I've got news for you," said Vince, "they already know. And if they don't, they soon will anyway."

"What do you mean?" asked Brad.

"I mean, we're fortunate to be living in an age that was prophesied a long time ago – a day when people's sins are shouted from the housetops. You can't keep anything hidden for long anymore. Not with the Internet and all. And that might not be such a bad thing. Sometimes the very worst parts of ourselves dwell in depths of darkness and secrecy. That's where they thrive. Getting them out into the light lets you see how small they really are. After a while, they all just shrivel up and blow away. People do eventually forgive and forget."

"I don't know," said Brad doubtfully.

"That was one Hell of a world we used to live in, Brad – in many ways. And now it's time to start letting all that darkness go and start moving on to the next stage. It's a lot brighter and happier there."

"Well, what do we do there?"

"Come on. First, we're going to get our rejuvenated, immortal, resurrected bodies back. Pretty soon you'll have a brand-new set of vocal chords, and you'll be singing all those super high notes again. There are millions of bands out there all hoping you'll join them on stage for a number or two. Even Eljay's been asking about you. He's hoping you might sing with his band here in the next little while."

"Eljay?"

"You know – *Him* – with a capital *H*."

"What??"

"Yeah, not only that, but he plays blues guitar like you wouldn't believe."

Chapter 13: The Big Maple Leaf in the Sky

*Music is a higher revelation
than all wisdom and philosophy.*
Ludwig van Beethoven

i. On the Road

Transcript: CBS Evening News with Scott Pelley - August 17, 2012

Pelley: Steve Hartman meets "A Different Drummer" when we come back.

[Commercial intro: Tonight's "On the Road" segment is sponsored by ...]

[Cut to commercial]

Pelley: Finally, tonight – There are some who are said to 'march to the beat of a different drummer.' Steve Hartman may have met that different drummer – On the Road.

Hartman: You may remember our recent story about Joyce Elmore, the blind piano teacher from Grandyle Village, New York. She didn't think her story was all that interesting – at least not compared to that of a one-armed drum instructor she knows. In a rare venture north of the border we headed to St. Catharines, Ontario to meet a man of amazing talent and generosity – Neil Peart.

[Shot of Peart with student]

Peart: Two, … three, … four. That's it. That's it! You've got it.

Hartman: Fans of science fiction and fantasy literature may already be familiar with the name Neil Peart. He's the author of several cult classics like *The Tobes of Hades*, *The Bastille's Blade*, and *Hour of the Necromancer*. But despite this success, Neil isn't your average celebrity.

Peart: I keep a pretty low profile. And when I am approached by the occasional fan, they suddenly seem unsure about asking for an autograph, a photo, or even a handshake.

Hartman: And that's alright with Neil. Living in the limelight was never one of his aspirations, even though he was going places as a talented, energetic drummer long before he was a writer. Dreams of musical success in the rock world seemed to be within his grasp.

[Shot of Peart, fast-paced drum solo]

Hartman: If you close your eyes and just listen, you'd never know this remarkable drummer only has one hand. But that wasn't always the case.

[Close-up of Peart in conversation]

Peart: I was twenty-one years old – on my way to an audition with two guys from a band called Rush, incidentally. You may have heard of them. Anyway, they needed a drummer to keep their trio going. I don't recall the accident, but when I awoke in the hospital, I immediately sensed a loss. Not pain so much, but balance and symmetry were missing. I knew. I just knew before anyone said anything, that I'd lost my right arm – or a good part of it anyway.

Hartman: Because of a drunk driver, Neil's percussion career came to an abrupt halt. But undaunted, he immediately put his remaining hand to work – writing those fiction books he is now famous for.

[Shot of Hartman in conversation with Peart]

Hartman: But now you're a drummer again. And not only a drummer, but an instructor as well. How did all that come about?

Peart: I missed it. I missed everything about drumming – the focus, the concentration, the precision. Plus, it's a great workout! It keeps me physically active.

[Shot of Peart drumming in his home studio]

Hartman: Twelve years after the car accident, Neil decided to give it another try.

Peart: It took about two years to get the mechanics exactly right – trying to find expansion springs with just the right tension and flex.

[Close-up of the prosthetic with drumstick attachment]

Hartman: Fitted to his right arm is a custom-made prosthetic device with an extended drumstick attached to it. Neil designed and fabricated it himself – proof that there's more to his genius than just writing and drumming.

Peart: I'll probably never be as good as I once was, but I did get back into drumming, and it feels great.

Hartman: Not only is Neil working his drumkit again but for the past sixteen years, he's been teaching young students from a local youth program as well.

Peart: There was a time, in my younger days, when I seemed more focused on myself – my own progress and creativity. But I've found life feels best when giving back to others. To family. To friends. To community. To life itself. It's very satisfying.

[Shot of Peart instructing student]

Peart: Okay, let your left hand relax a little. Let the stick do its work. Yes, like that!

Hartman: At any given time, Neil has five or six students that he mentors throughout the week. And what's more, he doesn't charge a single Canadian penny for these services.

[Shot of Hartman in conversation with Peart]

Hartman: So, you teach these kids for free?

Peart: Why not? Why not help build another generation of musicians? This world could use more of the magic that comes from music.

Hartman: And the world could use more magical artists and different drummers like Neil Peart. Steve Hartman. On the Road, St. Catharines, Ontario.

Pelley: That's the CBS Evening News for tonight. I'm Scott Pelley. Goodnight.

ii. Didacts and Parents

Brampton, Ontario – April 1996

"You've got some talent there, that's for sure," said Alex, recognizing the rarity of the moment. It wasn't like Julianne to stay sitting there at the table after dinner, especially to chat with her father.

"Yeah, I do have some talent, and I want to do something with it," she responded emphatically.

Alex loved his daughter, Julianne, but there always seemed to be some slight irritation between the two of them. The thoughts and words of her two older brothers were as familiar and comfortable to Alex as his own. Julianne, on the other hand, seemed to come from some strange, foreign planet. Ever since she was born, her logic and perceptions left Alex continuously baffled – at least until she turned sixteen more than a year earlier. That was when Julianne started doing and saying things that sounded more and more familiar to Alex.

It took a few months before it dawned on him that Julianne was becoming more and more like a version of himself at that age. This emerging recognition and its increasing familiarity only left Alex feeling less and less comfortable, however. He did not like the idea of seeing his youth, with all its blissful ignorance, its misplaced enthusiasm, its mistakes, its miscalculations, and the endless disappointment of its dashed hopes, paraded in front of him all over again.

"Well, sure," said Alex, trying to sound encouraging, "music's a great hobby, and–"

"I'm not talking about a hobby," interrupted Julianne. "I'm not talking about coming home every night from a job I don't like and strumming my guitar in the corner for a couple hours just to shake off what a bad work day it has been."

Alex took the jab directly and sat quietly for a moment, acknowledging that she had just described him accurately.

"So, what are you saying then? What is it you want to do?" he asked.

"I can make it. I can make it on my own! We're pulling in about two hundred and eighty dollars a night with our band and–"

"Wait a second. Two hundred eighty dollars a night?" asked Alex. "The whole band or each of you?"

"Each of us," answered Julianne, "and that's not counting–"

"How many nights a week? Two maybe? That's not even enough to–"

"We can do it! I know we can make it."

"And what about school?"

"What do you mean? I'm almost done with school!"

"I'm talking about *after* high school. What about college?"

"We've talked about this before. I don't see why I need to go to college. Why can't I just make a living being a musician?"

"Because it's not easy being a musician. Education gives you something to fall back on, in case–"

"In case of what? Are you saying I'm going to fail?"

"No! I'm just saying it's always a good idea to have a Plan B."

"Yeah, well, what if the energy and focus I put into Plan B takes away the energy and focus I need to make Plan A successful? I certainly would need a Plan B at that point, wouldn't I, because Plan A would fail. You talk about a Plan B, but that's just a self-fulfilling prophecy – of failure!"

"But you need–"

"You're not listening!" exclaimed Julianne. "Can you name any tightrope walkers?"

"What?"

"Yeah, name a famous tightrope walker. Just think of the first name that comes into your head."

"Well, there's the Wallenda family," said Alex. "I don't know any others."

"Yeah, there's hundreds of tightrope walkers performing at circuses and stuff all over the world, and nobody knows their names. And the reason is, they all use safety nets and–"

"Hang on! Hang on!–"

"The reason you know the Wallenda name is because they're famous. They're famous for being the best. They have to be the best because they don't use safety nets. They have no Plan B!"

"Well I have news for you. Every once in a while, a Wallenda falls to his death. And as your parents, all we want to do is see that you–"

"You're not listening to–"

"Look, Honey, trying to become a successful guitar player is hard enough if you're a man, but if you're a–"

"What are you saying? Women can't be–"

"Forget tightrope walkers. How about if you try naming some women guitar players off the top of your head?"

"What about Nancy Wilson? What about Joan Jett? Or Susan–"

"Yeah, that's what I'm saying," answered Alex. "Two. Two big names is all. I'm just trying to say, look at the reality of – I mean, you just don't see too many–"

"What about Susan Tedeschi?"

"Never heard of her. So, you're saying you're as good as Nancy Wilson?"

"Well, maybe not yet, but how am I ever going to get there if I'm not out there playing guitar all the time? How am I going to get there if I'm going to college instead? Or if I'm working on some Plan B? Anyway, what about that tune I had you listen to the other day?"

"What about it?"

"You said you liked it," said Julianne.

"Yeah?"

"Yeah, you said it was nice guitar. Well, that was Susan Tedeschi playing blues guitar on that track. And that's what I want to do – play blues guitar. And if she can do it – if she can cut an album and tour – then so can I."

"Well, that would be great, but we just think it would be good to get the security of a college education, that's all."

"What about you? You didn't go off to college. Did you even finish high school??"

"No, I didn't go to college. That's my whole point. And now I've got this crappy construction job where–"

"Yeah, you didn't go to school because you went off after your guitar-playing dreams. You got to go touring. You got to make a couple albums. You changed your last name to Lifeson. All that stuff – that's what I want to do."

"Oh, so, you want to end up in a job that has nothing to do with music? Like me?"

"What do you mean? You don't understand what I'm saying!"

"You think I don't know what you're going through? You don't think I have felt like this myself before?"

"Oh, I know you've felt exactly this way before. I've heard this conversation before, Alex Zivojinovich!"

"Hey, what do you mean by that, young lady?" asked Alex.

"I saw your movie. In school."

"What?"

"We watched your movie in Social Studies class today. After seeing it, I thought for sure you'd understand. I thought you knew what it's like to have dreams of pursuing music. And now you're giving me all this parental, Plan B crap. I thought you would–"

"Wait a minute here. What movie are you talking about?"

"You don't know? Like you've never seen that movie about a bunch of Canadian teens stuck in a farmhouse for a couple months? And there's this long-haired kid named Alex Zivojinovich, who wants to play the guitar, but his parents keep talking him down and telling him he's not good enough, telling him that he won't last in the music business. Well, maybe he could have been great if he never listened to them!"

"Oh…that movie," said Alex quietly. He knew full well what Julianne was talking about – a documentary film he had appeared in long ago when he was not much older than she was. Alex felt like smiling over the memory but wasn't sure that would help steer his daughter in a more practical direction. He managed to keep a straight, concerned look on his face.

"That's why we're sitting here having this talk," Julianne went on, "because I thought you, of all people, would understand."

"I do understand, Honey, maybe better than you think, because I have had that experience. I have been through it all already. I mean, yeah, I did get to do some touring. Geddy and I got to put out a couple albums, sure. But they didn't really take off like we thought they would. I had a family to feed, and music just wasn't paying the bills. Things just didn't work out like I hoped they would when I was your age."

"Maybe things didn't work out because you quit! Maybe you quit because you listened to your folks telling you that you wouldn't make it in the music business. Maybe you didn't have enough energy to make your Plan A become a success because you let yourself be distracted by your parents' Plan B negativity. Maybe your folks were right because you proved them right. Well, I'm not going to let myself get distracted by your doubts about me. I'm going to prove you wrong!"

Julianne left the room in a fury, ran upstairs and slammed her bedroom door.

"I hope you do," said Alex under his breath and with a slight smile that partially hid his inner sadness and regret. He wished he had ignored *his* parents when they said his musical talents would never take him anywhere.

iii. On the Cover of *Rolling Stone*

Excerpt from *Rolling Stone* article, *A Funny Thing Happened on the Way to the Quorum: The Happenstance Success of Quorum Bassist Geddy Lee*, Marcus Dean-Wayman, June 1981

"So, I've got these swimming trunks on, and they're basically two-toned – black & yellow stripes. I guess maybe that's an attractive color combo for bees (laughs). And, well, I can sort of subconsciously hear buzzing like some kind of group bee activity is going on nearby, and I can see bees flying around, but I'm not really thinking about it or noticing anything unusual. Anyway, I'm standing there next to the hotel pool, and I have no idea that bees are starting to land on the backside of my swimming trunks – *en masse* – you know? It seems like everyone else knew what was going on though and they got quiet all of a sudden like there's some old case of nitroglycerin nearby that could go off with the slightest bump. They're all scared that I'm going to get stung to death or something.

"Then Nancy quietly says, 'Don't move,' and I freeze, 'cause the tone in her voice is so serious and soft at the same time. I was just riveted. So, I said, 'What's going on?' and she says, 'Just don't move. You've got some bees on you.' And right then I feel this tickling on my back, just above the waistband on my trunks. I was starting to flinch a little, and Nancy says, 'Don't move,' again.

"And now I'm starting to remember getting stung on the arm by a bee or a wasp or something when I was a little kid, and it was like two stings in a row, less than half an inch apart. And the neighbor guy next door hears me crying, and you know, he's trying to help me laugh it off, saying, 'Wow! That looks like a snakebite! Are you sure some rattlesnake didn't get you?' And all that might have helped except those two stings were starting to swell, and I had this raised pair of bumps on my arm, and it scared me. I mean, it got better soon enough, but all that left an impression on me as a little kid.

"And now here it is more than twenty years later, and all of a sudden I've got my rear end covered in bees and they're starting to go up my back. I'm thinking, if they start stinging me I could swell all up and die from some allergic shock reaction or something. And I'm not joking when I say it was only a matter of seconds before my back is completely covered with bees. I look over at Nancy, and she's got this look on her face like I'm about to be shot by a firing squad. The swarm on me is just getting bigger and bigger, and then it starts circling around the front of my torso and moving up towards my neck, and I'm thinking, this is it, I'm going to die in just a matter of minutes here.

"And I've got two options going through my mind at this point. One is to keep following Nancy's plea and stay put, and the other is to just run for it and maybe try to jump in the pool before I get stung too many times. And right in the middle of this mental debate, it was like I heard a voice telling me to be still. I say 'voice,' but it was more like a powerful impression, although the words seemed quite clear and distinct. 'Be still.' And there was a moment of ironic humor in that, you know, with the word *be* sounding just like the word *bee* and I kind of started laughing to myself about that.

"But anyway, the effect of that voice was just so strong and calming and reassuring, and it instantly turned the situation around. I mean, one minute, I'm terrified about dying, and now I'm all relaxed and smiling and chuckling to myself. And the feeling is electric. If you're ever able to get a bunch of swarming bees to land on you, it's nothing but energy – this collective vibration that's just incredible to experience. Everyone at the pool is wondering if I've gone nuts, 'cause I'm just standing there covered in bees, but now I'm smiling, and I softly say to Nancy, 'It's okay. I'm fine. Don't worry.'

"And I got all that out before my face was completely covered, and I'm just amazed at the peaceful calm I'm feeling. The voice that said, 'Be still' filled me with that reassurance. But I did have one concern. I've got this famous huge nose, you know? And I'm thinking, that's it. If these bees start crawling inside my nose, it's over. I won't be able to handle that. I mean, I won't be able to breathe for one thing, obviously. But they never did. They never explored those nostrils of mine, and so I'm just breathing away, all the while covered almost completely with this electrified, buzzing mass. I stood like that for a couple minutes. It was a magical, mystical experience. I didn't get stung once. Somebody had called emergency, but by the time the paramedics arrived, something happened with the bees, and they all took off to some other place. I don't know why.

"So, back in the hotel room a few hours later, I'm still pondering this whole strange experience, wondering what it was that got me feeling so calm in the middle of that swarm. And just out of curiosity I crack open a copy of Gideon's Bible there in the room, and it randomly opens to the Psalms, and the first words I see are, 'Be still, and know that I am God.' And I'm just floored by that. I mean, as an atheist and all, I wasn't inclined to take the God idea seriously. But I couldn't deny what I had heard there out by the pool, and I couldn't deny the complete sense of comfort and peace that came over me. It was unreal.

"And interestingly, I was also suddenly feeling that same kind of peace about my musical future. I wasn't worried about it anymore. I just strongly sensed that things would work out. I mean, once John [Rutsey] left Rush, Alex [Lifeson] and I were never able to find a drummer we felt good about. And then Alex quits the music business altogether, and I'm left scraping for session work here and there for a few years. I didn't know if I was going to be able to keep going like that. Anyway, later that evening – the same day as that bee incident – the phone rings and it's Keith [Moon] on the other line, inviting me to join his new project. And that was the beginning of the Quorum band. You know the rest of the story so far. It's been nothing but success from then on. You know, I'm not religious or anything, but I do feel a certain familiarity with God now. Like, he knows who I am and that he is interested in my musical progress."

iv. All the Worlds Are a Stage

"Not too shabby for a first-time effort, don't you think?" I asked after the show. I had never put a reunion concert together on my own before and was looking for a little validation from my mentor.

"I must admit, Lawrence, I am impressed!" said Giselle with a big smile. "How did you ever manage to get Three Dog Night back together like that? Weren't some of them not even on speaking terms for a long while?"

"Maybe that was true at one point," I said, "but they were actually pretty enthused about performing as a group again. Finding them all though – that was the hard part. Chuck Negron and Floyd Sneed were both about twelve galaxies apart!"

"Well, I have to say the band looked like they were genuinely thrilled to be there. And I don't know if their harmonies ever sounded better than they did at this show. The crowd was ecstatic!"

"It doesn't hurt to float a little borium quadroxide gas out into the auditorium," I said with a sly grin. "It has a way of solidifying the core sound and softening its edges."

"Where did you learn about borium quadroxide?" asked Giselle, even more impressed with my resourcefulness.

"A little trick Smalls taught me a while back," I replied. "Try it with Anita Baker's voice, and you can melt the hearts of the most hardened criminals. They just start crying all of a sudden."

"Really?" said Giselle. "I wonder why Smalls never told me about this?"

"It's sort of a newer discovery. It hasn't really been tried much with Earth music until recently – probably because borium quadroxide gas is super toxic to mortals. It works just great in a Stage Three environment though. Anyway, if you thought the Three Dog Night show was good, wait 'til you hear the next band I'm putting together."

"Supertramp? Kansas?"

"Not quite yet, no. It's no one you've ever heard of before."

"Oh yeah? Try me."

"No, what I mean is, it's kind of a new group. Ta'a Neh and I have been working on getting them together for a while now."

"They're from Earth?"

"Yeah, they were Canadians – all three of them. Two of them have played together before and even put out a couple of LPs. Have you ever heard of a band called Rush?"

"Let's see," paused Giselle. "Aren't they the ones that did the *Powerhouse* album?"

"Yep. That was Rush's second and final album. It was pretty good, but it never really got the airplay that it should have. Anyway, Rush broke up a short time after that and a few years later, their bassist, Geddy Lee, went on to join Keith Moon's band, Quorum."

"Quorum?! I love those guys!" squealed Giselle. "Especially the *Bound with Chords* album!"

"Well, then you'll love this new band we're putting together. So, we've got Geddy Lee and guitarist, Alex Lifeson, from Rush back together and we're teaming them up with this amazing drummer we found named Neil. He lost part of his arm there on Earth and never went very far with his drumming. But now that he's all back in one piece, you should hear him. He's making up for lost time!"

"So, are they still going to be called Rush?"

"No. It's basically a new band with new material. More of a progressive rock sound. They're going with the name 'Maple Leaf Trio' – you know, keeping that Canadian theme going. Neil's quite a writer, so he's working on lyrics and stuff. I think they're going to be great!"

"It sounds like it," said Giselle. "But, now wait. Is Geddy Lee going to be their lead singer again?"

"Yeah. Why?" I asked.

"Well," answered Giselle, "I know he never sang lead for Quorum, but if I recall correctly, his voice didn't always get the most positive reviews."

"That's true," I answered, "but nobody ever heard him sing with a little borium quadroxide in the air either!"

******

Yasgur Amphitheater, Deinousse – Earth-year 2112

"Ladies and gentlemen! Will you please welcome, from Earth – the Maple Leaf Trio!"

There was enthusiastic applause from the crowd as spotlights focused on the three energetic Canadian musicians. The band immediately charged into *Monkey Business*, *Bastille Day*, and *The Snowdog*, one after the other. Before the thunderous applause completely died down, Geddy Lee addressed the audience.

"Good evening! Thank you, Planet Deinousse – The place with a Great White North *and* a Great White South so close together! But, what a warm welcome and what a beautiful outdoor amphitheater. It's a pleasure to be here, and we hope you enjoy some new music that we've put together for you tonight. Our next tune is a long one, hearkening back to ancient fabled stories from our home world. It's a story of wealth and pleasure and hoped-for immortality. We were going to call it *Xanadu* – but that name was already taken, wasn't it Olivia?" Geddy asked, with a slight chuckle.

Together with the crowd, Olivia Newton-John clapped her hands and gave a delightful little laugh herself from her seat in the third row. Sitting close behind her were Smalls and William Shakespeare.

"All the worlds are a stage, aren't they, Bill?" said Smalls with a nudge of his elbow. No longer balding, but still sporting a beard and mustache, Bill managed a very slight smile, along with a closed-lipped, stuttered, throaty hum – a sound several steps away from a genuine laugh. Bill had heard that one before. At least forty-thousand times before.

125

Chapter 14: Me and Greg

*After death, when my flesh has
decayed, yet in my body, I will see God.*
Job

There are so many invisible waves of energy – gravity, magnetism, radioactivity, and even those "spooky" connections between distant bits of matter that Einstein once argued couldn't or shouldn't exist. All those forces, combined with many others, can be manipulated and employed, harnessed and structured as data – information that can quickly breeze through the eternities. Sent and received on a timeless wavelength known to some as "the grid," the data is easily read and understood by the aware and the literate, just like paper and ink. Those on Earth who could barely grasp the basics of this literacy were said to engage in telepathy. Others who were sent grand panoramic visions through the grid were called prophets.

But for many of us who have moved beyond our earthly lives and are now clothed with immortality, this processing of information through the grid is no more remarkable than using some earthly wireless devices. Except that it *is* more remarkable – infinitely more! Anyway, it was through the grid that I got word from Smalls who was far, far away at that moment. He gave me the assignment to welcome a recent arrival.

"I can't believe my luck!" I responded when I heard who I was to greet.

"Luck has nothing to do with it, Lawrence," came the reply from Smalls. "This one's all yours."

Greeting someone as they enter the Third Stage is a great honor and a privilege. Not everyone gets invited to perform this service. Probably because it's a delicate matter, and you want to help get people off to the best possible start in the eternities. It's not unlike the welcoming of a newborn baby. Or a better analogy is being at a friend's hospital bedside when they awaken from general anesthetic. They don't know where they are at first and you kind of help reintroduce them to their surroundings with mild conversation about the past and their future.

When I entered the reception room, I found my charge lying there on a long sofa with his eyes still closed as expected. It would be a while before he came to, and I just sat there nearby, contemplating the historical singularity of this moment – this once-in-eternity chance for me.

The young man began to stir, and I watched for his eyes to open. When they finally did, I softly said, "You made it. Welcome back!"

He turned his face more my direction and began focusing his eyes on me. "Uh, thanks," he replied, sounding very groggy and disoriented, but with a smoothness to his youthful voice that took both of us by surprise. "Where am I?"

"This is the reception room," I said. "You just passed through."

"Passed through where?"

"Back to here, where we used to live. You're not in mortality anymore." He looked at me intently, straining to comprehend what I had just said. "Look at your hands," I said.

The young man lifted his arms before him and examined both sides of his hands. He was not able to fully grasp how they had suddenly come to look so youthful. To him, everything seemed like a dream from which he was not particularly anxious to awaken.

"You're one of the lucky ones," I added. "Came straight through resurrection without having to wait at all." He still looked pleasantly dazed as if enjoying this dream with all its peculiar notions and talk.

"By the way, I'm Lawrence. And you're Greg, aren't you? We've met a couple times before."

"I'm sorry," he said, looking past his hands. "I can't–"

"Don't worry," I said, "it will all come back to you soon enough. You'll start remembering everything. Even things you've long forgotten. But right now, just relax and take it easy. There's plenty of time. In fact, there's so much time here, it's like it doesn't exist at all."

There followed a lull in the conversation while Greg looked around the room and its furnishings, absorbing the beauty of it all. Sometimes his eyes would close again for a few moments as if he were taking short naps.

"Where's Dave?" he suddenly asked, with his eyes fully open.

"Oh, he's here," I said reassuringly, "and Steve is here too. You'll get a chance to meet up with them here soon."

"What about Larry?"

"He's on his way. And when he gets here, you'll have the whole band back together again."

"Good. Good," said Greg with a slight smile. "And my family's here too, right?"

"Yep. Well, the ones that arrived here before you. The others will be along in a while. Sounds like you're starting to remember some things."

"Yeah, I guess so," he said, still smiling softly, taking another look at his youthful hands. The skin on the backs of them was tight, elastic, and smooth, with no age spots to be found. Curiously though, his fingertips – especially on his left hand – were dressed in a thicker type of skin, almost like callouses, except with no signs of dryness or cracking. "So, you say we've met before?" he asked.

"A couple times, yeah. You probably wouldn't re-member me just yet. Besides, that last time we met I looked a bit older than I do now," I said with a grin. "Just like you looked older than you do now." Greg gently ran his fingers down his cheeks checking for loose, jowly skin and found none.

"We met by accident I guess, at a deli in Berkeley," I said. "My friend Sue was really ill, and you went with me to pay her a visit. Remember that?"

"Sort of. Was she wearing a turban or something?"

"Yeah, a head covering. She had lost all her hair with the chemo treatments. And you sang her a couple of songs that evening."

"And then she…," his voice drifted off with the added remembrance.

"Yeah, she's here now. Been here a while. Got all her hair back and everything!"

"Wow, that's something. So, everyone here is–"

"Yep, all the re-embodied ones anyway, like you and me – recaptured in their prime. No sickness, no suffering, no more death and dying."

"Amazing," said Greg as he tried to comprehend it all.

"It sure is," I said.

"So, … what do we do here?"

"Pretty much anything and everything!" I said enthusiastically. "But you should know, there's a lot of music here. Good stuff too. Stuff you couldn't even dream about back on earth."

"But there's still rock, right?"

"Oh, yeah. There's a lot of people here looking forward to seeing you play again."

"A lot? Like who?"

"You thought you had fans back on Earth? Man, multiply that number four or five billion times, and then you'll start understanding what I mean."

"No way. How could that ever be?"

"Well, it's because you haven't really had a chance to build up a large following yet. But you know, you just keep working at it, and after a while, you could really have a decent sized fan base here."

I was messing with Greg a little, trying to gradually stretch and stimulate his awakening mind with an idea of how immense eternity is – like splashing water on a kid's legs before they enter a chilly pool. But everything I said was true. From across countless galaxies and eons, Greg had unknowingly developed billions and billions of fans, and all of them looked forward to the chance of hearing him and his band play once again.

Greg sat there dumbfounded and perplexed. I decided to bring him back down to earth, so to speak, with some talk of things he was more familiar and comfortable with.

"You remember the Keystone club in Palo Alto?" I asked.

"The Keystone, yeah. A lot of gigs there," he answered, still very hazy, but regaining more of his memory.

"Well, one night you had Little Roger and his band open for you guys."

"Little Roger ... and the Goosebumps. I remember them," he said, nodding. "Didn't they do *Stairway to Gilligan's Island*?"

"That's them."

"And you say they opened for us at the Keystone?"

"The one in Palo Alto, yeah – not the one in Berkeley. Anyway, it wasn't the Goosebumps that night. It was the Dots."

"Oh yeah, the Dots. Little Roger and the Dots. I remember that now."

"Well, by chance I met their bass player and somehow got myself invited to do some roadie work at their next gig. And you know what? A few nights later, they were opening for Greg Kihn at the Keystone in Palo Alto!"

"How 'bout that?" said Greg, forgetting the eternities for a moment and getting into our conversation.

"Yeah, I couldn't believe it. I mean, I had seen you guys perform there a few times before, and now I was getting a free backstage pass! And I'm thinking, this is the greatest thing in the world, right?" Greg nodded and laughed along with my growing enthusiasm in telling this tale.

"And so," I went on, "I got to meet everyone backstage and all that – Dave and Steve and Larry and Little Roger –

and I'm having the time of my life, you know? But I didn't get to meet Greg Kihn."

"Why was that?" he asked.

"I don't know. You were busy talking to other folks, I guess. Anyway, at one point I'm standing there in the hallway behind the stage, and these two guys are moving toward me. And one is sort of walking backward as they're talking together and he accidentally bumps into me and steps on my foot. And the guy turns around suddenly, very apologetic, and says, 'I'm sorry," then goes back talking to the other guy. And I'm stunned because you know who it was?"

"No. Who?" asked Greg.

"It was you!"

"Me? I stepped on your foot?"

"Yeah, and you turned around to say, 'Sorry,' and I'm thinking, 'I did it! I got to meet Greg Kihn in person!'"

"Wait a second," said Greg laughing. "You didn't steal a towel from me that night, did you?"

I silently hung my head in mock shame.

"Yeah, it's all coming back to me now," said Greg, and I could see him looking increasingly lively and energized as his mind began to adapt to this new phase of his existence.

"Well, that's good," I said, "because we're going to enter the main reception hall here soon. You'll get a chance to visit with relatives and friends you haven't seen for a while."

"Oh man, that sounds great," he replied, more alert now.

"What's more, we might even have you and the band play a few tunes at a little 'Welcome Back' party for you later on. What do you think about that?"

"Oh, I don't know," he said doubtfully. "It's been so long. Outta practice. And what about the equipment and all that?"

"Instruments, gear, lights, soundcheck – all taken care of. I even managed to sneak your favorite guitar on up here.

You know, the one with the small crack on the fingerboard? Besides, in a short while here, all your memory, talents, and abilities will be back better than ever, and you guys will sound great! Come on," I said, opening the door to the reception hall, "you've got loved ones to meet."

"But how will I find my way to the stage, later on?" Greg asked, still slightly disoriented.

"Oh, that's easy," I laughed as I recalled an old story about one of the band's early gigs in Hamburg, Germany. "Just follow the goat turds!"

Epilogue

Come on, dear brother, since the war is past,
For friends at first, are friends again at last.
Joseph Smith

Yasgur Amphitheater, Deinousse – Earth-year 2277

All eyes were drawn to what appeared to be a flying saucer high in the sky above. The movement of red and yellow lights near its outer rim suggested the disc was slowly rotating. Although unseen from below, smaller white lights near the top of its dome began to blink. Suddenly, there shot out a bright, direct, fixed beam of light from its undersurface. Far below, the beam illuminated an otherwise dark stage positioned before the vast crowd. Stepping into the spotlight was a tall, lanky figure sporting trademark, horn-rimmed glasses that he actually no longer needed to aid his sight.

"Good evening, ladies and gentlemen!"

There was extra cheering from those in the crowd who, with great surprise, recognized the figure.

"I'm Buddy Holly and–"

There was an eruption of shouting and applause that lasted for some time. All the while, the figure smiled, and nodded, and raised his hand in a slight, humble wave. It had been more than three Earth-centuries since the legendary music pioneer had made an appearance on stage.

"Thank you. Thank you very much. It has been a long time. Too long. It's wonderful to be here with all of you tonight. Again, I'm Buddy Holly, and I'd like to welcome you all to the second evening of this great event – the first of hopefully many EarthFest reunion concerts yet to come!"

There was another wave of cheering as the large audience recognized their great fortune in being able to attend this show live – in person.

133

"Was anyone able to attend last night's blues guitar opener?" Buddy asked.

There was a roar of affirmation from tens of thousands in the crowd.

"Wasn't that something? The legendary Stevie Ray Vaughn; the One and Only, Eljay; and of course, our headliner – The Tedeschi/Lifeson Band! Two of the greatest blueswomen you'll ever hear. How about that? You won't see another blues show like that for a couple more millennia," Buddy confidently declared to the delight of the crowd.

"And tomorrow night, for those who enjoy amazing vocals and harmonies, we've got Boston, Three Dog Night, the Little River Band, and Queen!" Loud bursts of applause followed each band's name.

"But tonight, we have a lineup that you'll never forget. How about Yes! Quorum! And of course, Led Zeppelin!!" The crowd's enthusiastic cheering and whistling seemed like it would never die down.

"Don't worry," said Buddy, "I haven't forgotten tonight's opening act – a band who needs no introduction. Let's hear it for our symphonic friends, originally from Birmingham, England!"

The crowd gave another roar as the spotlight from the craft above shrunk away to sudden darkness. Beneath a distant blanket of clouds, the rotation of the flying saucer's lights began to increase in speed. The craft loomed larger and larger as it began its long descent. The eerie sound of a choir began to emanate from the spaceship, followed by shrill, discordant strings. They were joined by a deep, tortured voice that started to moan in a language unfamiliar even to the English speakers in the crowd. Everyone sat riveted by the haunting sounds as the rotating disc slowly approached and then finally settled onto the massive stage.

With bursts of vapor all about, the upper dome of the craft began to separate and rise above the lower disc. Bright white lights shone from inside the dome, illuminating the foggy space below, while the frantic music began to assume greater accord and unified rhythm. Seven shadowy, silhouetted figures and their instruments began to rise slowly and uniformly up through the bright light and fog inside the lower disc, revealing themselves as the music's performers. As the mist faded away, the crowd cheered loudly with recognition of the individual artists. A thin blue laser light drew an immense ELO logo across the clouds way above.

"It's *Fire on High!*" exclaimed Farookh.

"What?" asked Aboud.

"That's the name of this piece of music – *Fire on High!*" repeated Farookh. "Amazing! What an entrance!"

"And who are these musicians again?" asked Aboud.

"They're the Electric Light Orchestra. That's what the big E.L.O. up in the sky stands for. What do you think so far?"

"This is incredible," said Aboud in utter astonishment. "I've never, never seen anything even remotely like this. Not in Zanzibar, no."

Both Farookh and Aboud joined in the long, standing ovation that followed ELO's dramatic opening number. "Yes, I thought you might enjoy this, Aboud. But just wait until you see *our* band's entrance at tomorrow night's show!"

"I can't even imagine it!" exclaimed Aboud. "And you say your group is named Queen?"

"Yes, there are four of us, back together again. These reunion concerts are simply marvelous," said Farookh. "Now, do you see the guy up front there with the sunglasses and big hair? That's Jeff Lynne. And the drummer behind him? That's Bev Bevan. This is the first time those two have played on stage together since their Earth days. They weren't even speaking to each other for the longest time."

"I can tell you, reconciliation is a beautiful thing, my friend," said Aboud. "Forgiveness is a beautiful thing. Thank you for coming to find me, Freddie. I was afraid all was lost forever."

"I thought all was lost for a while there too, my friend," came the reply. "It's quite ironic really, but the more you realize just how big forever is, the less room there seems to be for fears and enemies."

Chapter Notes

Chapter 1: Greg and Sue
Song lyrics found in this chapter come from the following copyrighted sources: *Roadrunner*, written by Jonathan Richman, and recorded on the 1979 album *With the Naked Eye* by The Greg Kihn Band; *For You*, written by Bruce Springsteen, and recorded on the 1977 album *Greg Kihn Again* by Greg Kihn; *Remember*, written by Greg Kihn, and recorded on his 1978 album, *Next of Kihn*.

Chapter 2: No Escape from Reality
Did a young Parsee named Farookh once kill a man in Zanzibar? Did he actually put a gun against someone's head and pull the trigger? Is this the real life? Or, is this fantasy? Regarding *Bohemian Rhapsody*'s lyrics, its composer, Freddie Mercury, once extended an invitation for people to "make up their own minds as to what it says to them." That invitation opens imagination's door to all kinds of thoughts, theories, and even wildly speculative fiction.

Chapter 3: Rock of Ages
To provide hope and comfort in this life, the concept of resurrection has been conveyed to mortals for millennia by prophets from a variety of religions and philosophical backgrounds. Not surprisingly, the very existence of these prophets, along with their words and teachings about the resurrection, has been dismissed by most scholars as myths and fables. Even the vast majority of those professing faith in these teachings often do not comprehend them or take them literally. Such was the case with Saul. He was well versed in the words of Job, Daniel, and Isaiah, all of whom spoke quite plainly about the eventual reuniting of body and spirit in the afterlife. And yet, the concept of resurrection was unacceptable to Saul prior his wondrous encounter on the road to Damascus. That encounter has also been dismissed by modern-day scholars who are completely unaware of the

many resurrected beings who walk among us undetected – especially at art exhibits and musical performances.

Chapter 4: Devils, Dullards, and Deities
In the early 1990s, journalist Ron Reagan Jr. conducted a lengthy televised interview with Charles Manson, would-be musician and convicted mastermind of several gruesome murders committed in 1969. That was the same year *Never Learn Not to Love* appeared on the Beach Boys' *20/20* album. The song was a re-working of Manson's tune, *Cease to Exist*. Manson passed away in prison in November of 2017, at the age of 83. The copyright for any *No Such Thing* lyrics found in this chapter belongs to John Mayer, as recorded on his 2001 album, *Room for Squares*.

Chapter 5: What Is and What Shall Never Be
There were only a few remaining show dates left on Led Zeppelin's 1977 U.S. tour schedule when suddenly, five-year-old Karac, son of frontman Robert Plant, took ill and died at home in England. The Oakland, California concert on Sunday, July 24th marked the last time the band would ever play outside of Europe. The copyright for any lyrics of *The Rain Song* found in this chapter belongs to Jimmy Page and Robert Plant, as recorded on the 1973 album, *Houses of the Holy*.

Chapter 6: Dregs of the Earth
Steve Morse was still very much alive at the time this highly fictional volume was written, the Dixie Dregs having just finished a successful 40th-anniversary tour with all original band members.

Chapter 7: Giant Silence
See Epilogue notes below.

Chapter 8: Karac and Giselle

In his late fifties, Lawrence wore a T-shirt that read, "I may be old, but I got to see all the cool bands in concert." Later in life, his daughter gave him a bumper sticker that read the same, and he proudly placed it on the back of his old, yellow Honda Civic. That was the day before he took the car in for repairs and called his friend, Eric, for a ride to work.

Chapter 9: Timeless

Lawrence recalled his grandfather once saying, "I've had this same pickaxe for over sixty years. I've replaced the head twice and the handle three times!" Lawrence used this story to explain to Giselle how some groups on Earth morphed into their own tribute bands. By way of legal stratagem, the group's name would be secured and perpetuated, while its talented sound-alikes would shamelessly tour and perform without a single original band member – to the delight of ignorant audiences everywhere. "If you played it right," mulled Giselle, catching on to some of the questionable practices used on Earth, "you could have more than one version of the same band touring the country at the same time." Lawrence nodded in agreement. "Worse things have happened," he said.

Chapter 10: Sound Chaser

Thanks to award-winning author Graham Mackintosh for bringing the history of the pitahaya fruit's "second harvest" to light in his inspiring true-life adventure, *Into a Desert Place*.

Chapter 11: Reminiscing

Lyrics from *Down Under* mentioned in this chapter were written by Colin Hay and Ron Strykert and were featured on the 1981 album, *Business as Usual*, by Men at Work. Glenn Shorrock and the other members of the Little River Band enjoyed that first reunion show organized by Giselle – so much so that they performed over 27,000 more times during the next several millennia and even recorded the equivalent of forty-two more albums. Over and over they kept asking themselves why they hadn't gotten back together sooner.

Chapter 12: Up from the Deep

It would be difficult to find two talented musicians who could be defined more accurately as contemporaries. Vince Welnick and Brad Delp were born less than a year apart, and both brought their own lives to an unfortunate end less than a year apart. Neither were permitted to regain their physical, resurrected bodies immediately, allowing them time to more fully understand and appreciate the great gifts of life and immortality.

Chapter 13: The Big Maple Leaf in the Sky

i. On the Road

Following the release of Rush's first album, the band performed live for about four months until drummer, John Rutsey, could no longer continue due to health concerns. Bassist, Geddy Lee, and guitarist, Alex Lifeson, tried out several replacements but none seemed suitable. Adding to their discouragement, the most potentially promising drummer, Neil Peart, mysteriously failed to show up for his audition and never answered any calls. After several months of forced hiatus for the band, Lee and Lifeson were able to talk drummer, John Rutsey, back into the studio for a second Rush LP called *Powerhouse*, which was released in early 1975. The album was popular with the band's relatively small fan base but failed to significantly surpass the sales of the first LP. Rutsey reached a final breaking point with his health, and the band did not support the *Powerhouse* album with a promotional tour. Rush dissolved a short time later with a much discouraged, Alex Lifeson, returning home to a construction job, and Geddy Lee heading to Los Angeles hoping to pick up work as a session musician.

ii. Didacts and Parents

The referenced film was a 1972 documentary titled, *Come on Children*, produced and directed by Allan King. In the early 1970s, King gathered ten Canadian teenagers to live in an isolated farmhouse for ten weeks, giving them a chance to consider their lives and futures without parental constraints. Among those teens was a young guitarist, Alex Zivojinovich, who was not yet known by his stage name, Alex Lifeson. During this documentary, nineteen-year-old Alex has a spirited discussion with his visiting parents who insist that his guitar talents, and his young band named Rush, will never take him anywhere. Ignoring similar parental suggestions, Julianne Zivojinovich would assume her father's former stage name, Lifeson, and eventually team up with Susan Tedeschi. Together they formed the most influential blues guitar duo ever known.

iii. On the Cover of *Rolling Stone*

The band Quorum formed in late 1978, shortly after Keith Moon's recovery from a near-fatal drug overdose. Members of Moon's former group, The Who, considered him too unreliable after this crisis and replaced him with Faces drummer Kenney Jones. While working to get his health back in order, Keith Moon defiantly set about launching a new solo album right away. In what was initially supposed to be a six-week side project, Moon was soon joined by four others – guitarist Robert Fripp of King Crimson, bassist Geddy Lee, Don Airey on keyboards, along with the vocal talents of David Coverdale. Once during an early recording session, someone reportedly hit a sour note causing a sound technician to humorously quip, "You could get arrested for that at The Quorum!" The name stuck to both the band and to what would become their eponymous first album. The name Quorum had reference to a New Orleans coffeehouse where, in 1964, police officers reportedly arrested several musicians for playing out of tune. As things turned out, Quorum was a surprisingly huge success. The five musicians stuck together for the next seven years, churning out four multi-platinum albums as they essentially assumed Led Zeppelin's former throne. John Bonham called Quorum, "the most unlikely of quintets to compose and perform such stratospheric pieces of music."

iv. All the Worlds Are a Stage
The Maple Leaf Trio tune that might have been named Xanadu sounded nothing at all like the one Olivia Newton-John once recorded. And, incidentally, the composition bore little resemblance to any known piece of music one might think of when recalling its title.

Chapter 14: Me and Greg
Greg Kihn was still very much alive at the time this highly fictional volume was written.

Epilogue Notes
The chilling, unintelligible words emanating from the Electric Light Orchestra spaceship as it descended were, "The music is reversible, but time is not!" – played backward, using a common 1970s studio technique known as backmasking. *Fire on High* was written by Jeff Lynne and was featured on ELO's 1975 album, *Face the Music*. By the time of the first EarthFest reunion concert on Deinousse, it was known that time *was* in fact reversible, but only from an observational standpoint. The past could be seen, but not changed or influenced or affected in any way. And so it was that Giant Silence's magical musical moment, interrupted at a wedding reception Earth-centuries earlier, could never be brought back exactly as it was or allowed to continue into further, other-worldly planes.

Acknowledgments

This work stands as an homage and an expression of gratitude to many bands and musicians who have made my life so much more enjoyable. I also wish to express thanks to Inda Berg, Bonnie Mortensen, Lawrence Newcomb, Jim Frost, and Joel Honea for keen insights and numerous valuable suggestions that vastly improved earlier versions of this book. Thanks go to B. Templeton for graphic arts help with the cover design. And, thanks to Mom for her persistent enthusiasm and encouragement of my creative efforts. I am also eternally grateful for the Rock of Ages, the Architect of the Resurrection, without hope in whom, "we are of all people most miserable."